MOONBRANCHES

Anne Rundle

Macmillan Publishing Company
New York

Macmillan Publishing Company
866 Third Avenue, New York, NY 10022
Collier Macmillan Canada, Inc.
First Edition
Printed in the United States of America

10 9 8 7 6 5 4 3 2 1

The text of this book is set in 12 point Electra.
Library of Congress Cataloging-in-Publication Data
Rundle, Anne. Moonbranches.
Summary: While spending the summer in the house
where her aunt is housekeeper in the early days of
World War I, fourteen-year-old Frances becomes involved
in the house's violent past when she is "visited" by
the long-dead twin of the owner's sinister son,
seventeen-year-old Martin.
[1. Supernatural—Fiction. 2. World War, 1914-1918—Fiction.
3. Mystery and detective stories] I. Title.
PZ7.R88827Mo 1986   [Fic]   86-5421
ISBN 0-02-777190-3

49004

For my grandchildren,
past, present, and future,
with my love

CHAPTER ONE

Frances could see the house from a long way off, nestling like a bird in the hollow above the crags. As she looked, she experienced a sensation of having seen it before. This should have been strange, but she'd experienced similar feelings in the past: She'd go somewhere and get a glimpse of a building or a setting she recognized, though it was impossible that she could previously have visited the place. Father called it precognition.

It was the same with Hallowes. It was as though she were a camera and something inside her had given a click the instant that the trap bowled around the last bend, fixing the image in her mind. She leaned forward, watching the late sun bathe the light-colored facade of the imposing structure, trying to forget the last glimpse of her father.

The man at her side said, "Well, there it is, miss."

She hadn't wanted to ask his name. At the station he'd looked severe with his harshly angled face and stiff uniform,

1

but now he looked relaxed, even smiling, though nothing could entirely alter the hardness of his features.

The drive wound upward through laurel, azalea, and rhododendron bushes grown huge and untamed, concealing the house until the trap bounded out from this claustrophobic tunnel to crunch on gravel.

Her heart gave a huge undisciplined leap as the building flashed into view, seeming to shiver as though about to crumble over the forecourt. The vehicle came to an abrupt halt, and the pillars and balustrades stopped their disconcerting wavering.

Hallowes became still and watchful, like a cat with a mouse. Then the huge front door opened to disgorge a small, stout figure in a black gown relieved by only a little white.

Frances got out of the trap and ran toward her aunt. Aunt Bessie was supposed to bear a great likeness to Queen Victoria. Frances, who'd seen portraits of the Queen, was forced to admit that her aunt's heavy-lidded eyes indeed resembled those of the King's dead grandmother, if paintings and miniatures could be believed.

"So there you are!" Aunt Bessie said. "We expected you sooner."

"The train was late, Mrs. Crabbe," the man told her, handing down the two portmanteaus that held Frances's possessions.

"You'd better come inside, then," Aunt Bessie ordered, not offering to kiss her niece, her pale eyes vexed. "I can't spare much time just now. I'll show you your room, and Robert can take your bags upstairs. Come, now."

Frances wasn't sure whether the vexation was directed toward herself or was only a reflection of her aunt's busy

2

schedule. Being housekeeper in so large an establishment must be harassing. Following the black-clad figure inside, Frances shuddered briefly as the chill of the big, shadowed hall closed about her.

Turning her head, she saw the brightness of the outside world through the rectangle of the doorway. Although she had taken only a few steps, she seemed as shut off from the sunlight as though she were in prison. A bell jangled tinnily, its rusty echoes lingering.

"Wait," Aunt Bessie commanded, as imperiously as that stout little queen might have done on some occasion on which she was *not* amused. "Wait here till I come back."

The hall became very quiet after she removed her stiffly corseted body with ponderous haste. The man called Robert had obviously gone to some other entrance with her two small bags. Frances imagined she heard harpsichord music, a bare thread of sound that might even originate from a different source. A waterfall?

She suddenly felt conspicuous, almost as if the dull amber eyes set in the antlered stag's head, fixed below a gloomy painting of incredible size, were capable of sight. She stared at it uneasily.

"Servants usually go to the side door," a soft, mocking voice remarked. Just for a moment Frances had an almost uncontrollable urge to reply to the moth-eaten head but was stopped by a burst of contemptuous laughter from the dimly lit staircase.

"You *are* stupid. But then, servants usually are. Fancy even thinking of holding a conversation with that."

Frances, her cheeks burning in the shadows, saw little more than a shape a fraction taller than herself. She had a

3

curious impression of a red glitter where the person's eyes should be, a reflection perhaps from a pane of colored glass above the door.

"I was told to wait here," she replied stiffly.

"Indeed?"

"Mrs. Crabbe asked me to."

"Oh, Crabby," the young voice said carelessly. "Are you to be taken on in the kitchen?"

Frances, with a strong conviction that her tormenter knew perfectly well who she was, said, "No, I am *not*. I am invited to stay here until I return to school in September. Mrs. Crabbe is my aunt."

"Oh, you must be Mama's war work. Every now and again she finds her conscience becoming troublesome. It's your turn to soothe it."

She could see the boy more clearly now that her eyes had become accustomed to the dimness. He had a pale, square face, dark curly hair, and a look of arrogance. If she'd met him under pleasanter circumstances, she'd have admitted that he was almost overpoweringly handsome. She wished she presented a more dashing image. Aristocratic young ladies wore more exciting clothes than her dark skirt and white blouse and the plain straw hat that perched precariously on her newly washed hair.

"I don't know anything about that. Do you always discuss your mother's conscience with complete strangers?"

"You do sound prunes and prisms." The boy smiled with a trace of satisfaction.

Frances knew she mustn't allow him to goad her into any indiscretion. Lady Hallowes had been more than kind, and Aunt Bessie would never forgive Frances if she caused a bad

4

impression, particularly on her first day. "Do I?" she asked distantly.

"You know you do." The boy sounded maddeningly sure of himself. How had he known about her urge to address the stuffed head? It was uncanny.

The straw hat began to slide off her thick, brown hair, and she caught it just in time. With every moment that passed, she felt more and more as if she'd stepped into the pages of *Alice in Wonderland*. There must be a word to describe her sense of a total loss of direction and identity.

"What's your name?" the boy asked, beginning to descend the stairs slowly and gracefully.

"Frances Lang," she answered, wishing that she didn't find him outwardly attractive.

"I think Mama will lose interest in you very quickly. She probably has an idealized picture of a pretty little miss, all golden ringlets and rosy lips. A helpless creature."

Before she could stop herself, Frances retorted, "I shouldn't be very interested in anyone who set such store by outward appearances."

"Oh, dear!" His eyes sparkled with pleased malice. "What would she say if she knew?"

"She won't unless you tell tales."

"You're a very direct person."

"No one would call you particularly devious," Frances observed, increasingly aware of travel fatigue and a longing to be rid of him. "I suppose you live here?"

"You sound as if you hope I'm a bird of passage. No such luck, Frances Lang. I'm Martin Hallowes."

"I did gather that. I just wondered if you went to boarding school."

5

"No. I had a tutor till recently. Papa has plans for me."
A scowl spoiled the attractive face. "At present I'm on holiday."

"You're going away?"

"Don't sound so hopeful! After all, how could we think of going anywhere when *you* were arriving?"

A rustling sound, accompanied by the sound of heavy footsteps, told Frances that her aunt was approaching.

"Her ladyship would like to see you, Frances. Oh, you're there, Master Martin." Frances had the impression that her aunt either disliked or mistrusted the boy. Perhaps she was aware of the nickname by which he called her. Aunt Bessie seemed totally devoid of humor and consequently much on her dignity. Not like Papa.

"I'll leave you to Mama's tender mercies," Martin Hallowes said mockingly, and crossed the marble-flagged entrance to disappear into the green-gold rectangle of the outside world.

"You *will* try to give a good impression, won't you?" Aunt Bessie panted, propelling herself along a dark, narrow hall studded with brown doors, rather like a seal through murky waters. Frances, resisting the temptation to say that she intended to create a scene of enormous flamboyance after which she'd be summarily ejected, agreed dutifully.

Aunt Bessie knocked at a door halfway along the passage.

A low-pitched voice called, "Come in."

Frances was ushered into a room in which the colors sage, black, and red predominated. Where a fugitive bar of light penetrated the heavy inner curtains of Nottingham lace, the gray-green wallpaper took on the semblance of lichen. A shaft of sunlight shone with extraordinary beauty through a greenish glass dome, inside which a miniature world of bark, grasses, and dried flowers was forever trapped.

6

Lady Hallowes stood up, shutting off the glow, and the wallpaper and the glass dome were reduced to shadows. She was slender, her pale, high-cheekboned face and dark red hair the image of Martin's. Her gown was a forest green with tight-fitting sleeves, a bodice trimmed with lace, and a skirt fuller than was presently fashionable but which suited her timeless elegance. A jet brooch and earrings were her only ornaments.

She came forward, her expression a little baffled, as though she'd been caught at a disadvantage, and Frances remembered Martin's rather cruel observations. The book she'd been reading lay on a low table, and Frances could see the title printed in gold: *The Poetic Works of Lord Byron*.

"You're taller than I expected," Lady Hallowes said, breaking some obscure spell.

"Am I?" Frances couldn't think of anything else to say. Studying the Turkish carpet, she sensed Aunt Bessie's silent exasperation.

"Frances would like to say thank you, your ladyship," her aunt said after a pause, stressing the two last words.

Frances flushed. "Oh, yes! I should, your ladyship."

"That's a good girl. How old are you? I've forgotten."

"Nearly fifteen."

"That's right. A year or two younger than Martin. When did your father—leave?" Lady Hallowes asked delicately.

Frances saw again the scene she could never forget: Papa in his khaki uniform, the peaked cap shading his eyes, his brass buttons sending off little flashes of brilliance. He'd nearly forgotten his kit bag as the train came in, shunting and puffing, a metallic dragon.

The station had gone all cloudy with steam, like a kitchen on apple-dumpling day, and the gray tendrils had drifted over

Papa's face at the open window of the grimy carriage.

"Yesterday." Already it seemed years ago. Her throat seemed to close.

"Goodness, you have been traveling a long time. And all on your own?"

"Mr. Taylor, that's Papa's friend who was seeing me off, gave something to the guard. Papa left him some money. The guard kept looking into the carriage to see if I was all right. I had a window seat, and there was so much to look at I really *was* all right." If you could be all right when your heart was breaking. . . .

"Yes, I'm sure you were. People can be so considerate." Martin's mother already sounded a little bored, and Aunt Bessie was fidgeting. "Now, I hope you'll enjoy your visit. Your aunt will tell you where your room is, and there's plenty to see outside. She has her own little sitting room where you can have your meals. I expect you're hungry."

"Yes, I am. Your ladyship."

"There's a good girl," her ladyship said again, dismissively.

"Come along then, Frances." Aunt Bessie gave a little bob and tugged at her niece's sleeve. Frances had been thinking that Lady Hallowes reminded her of the picture of Morgan le Fay in the Burne-Jones book Papa had given her on her last birthday. He'd bought it secondhand in London and she'd loved the haunting prints with their air of romantic mystery.

Following her aunt, Frances realized that she hadn't obeyed her strictures about making a proper impression. She hadn't addressed Lady Hallowes by her title every time she'd spoken, and when she had, it had been an obvious afterthought. But it took time to adapt to such grandeur and to giving people titles every time they were addressed.

Aunt Bessie swept along to the end of the passage and began to ascend a cramped staircase totally unlike the one at the front of the house. The small linoleum-covered steps seemed to go on forever, broken only by another hall that ran off into shadowy distances. At the next landing she deviated along an even narrower passage, followed by Frances, who was sure she could never find her way out of such a maze; she felt more like Alice than ever.

"Here you are," Aunt Bessie said. "You'll keep it tidy, won't you, and hang up your things straightaway, and wash your hands. I'll send Mary up to fetch you to my room for supper."

"Thank you."

"Your Papa was all right, was he?"

"Yes."

"It'll be fine, you'll see," Aunt Bessie muttered awkwardly as she bustled away. She seemed almost afraid of inviting confidences or affection—so unlike Papa that they seemd to have no connection one with another. Of course, Aunt Bessie had been the eldest of a large family of which the intervening children had, one by one, died in infancy, leaving only Papa, who was twenty years younger. It must have been very sad for their parents.

Frances thought of her long-dead grandparents as she took her few possessions out of the bags and hung them on the clothes hangers in the gloomy wardrobe. Her underwear and handkerchiefs were almost lost in the cavernous drawers of the dressing table, with its faintly tarnished mirror. The linoleum was polished to a cold gloss. It would be like walking over a frozen pond if she took off her boots and stockings.

Her thoughts reverted to her grandfather. She'd never really known her grandmother apart from a vaguely remembered visit when she was a small child. She'd been made to learn a song especially for her. Mother had rehearsed her so well that she could never forget the words even though she'd considered them rather silly.

Grandfather was a master plumber. Frances could never recall his not wearing a shiny, dark-gray suit and an old, black Homburg hat. Aunt Bessie had looked after him after Grandmother died, then she'd married Uncle Crabbe and Frances hadn't seen her till her own mother died of a fever.

Papa had been the clever one of the family, and was awarded a scholarship that led eventually to his obtaining a post as a schoolteacher. It was plain that Aunt Bessie had always resented Papa's greater intellect and poor Mama's prettiness. She could also have minded not having children. It was too much that her brother was next in line to becoming headmaster and also had a daughter.

Papa turned quiet after Mama died; he had saved up some money and sent Frances to an excellent boarding school. Uncle Crabbe also passed away—Aunt Bessie didn't subscribe to being too blunt about death—and Bessie had obtained a post as housekeeper in a modest establishment, being recommended to Lady Hallowes when her previous employers, who were friends of her ladyship, had been posted abroad just as Lady Hallowes required staff.

Frances, discovering that she was extremely tired, was tempted to lie down on the brass bed with its patchwork quilt, then remembered that she hadn't yet washed. The water in the large jug was faintly warm. Afterward, refreshed, she went belatedly to the small window, looking down on a diffusion of many greens in the depth of which water gleamed and the rounded whiteness of boulders shone like half-buried skulls. A sense of loneliness made the tears prick at her eyes.

Something moved close to the glass, tapping on the pane, but when she blinked there was nothing to be seen. Had a bird fluttered close to the pane? Perhaps she could entice it with crumbs on the sill and make a pet of it.

She became aware of her present solitude and that somewhere beyond the half-opened door a tap dripped.

Frances went out into the passage. Some yards away another door was ajar. Gray light exuded from the aperture. She tried to recall whether the door had been open when she first arrived on this floor, but the answer eluded her.

She went forward very softly and peered through the gap. It was silent but for the slowly falling droplets and a faint shuffling sound from above, as though someone with trailing skirts walked overhead. But who would wander about so quietly in the attic?

The hinges creaked as Frances pushed against the door, which moved stiffly to reveal a low-ceilinged, joyless room, porridge-colored at the top and dark brown at the bottom, with a dividing border halfway up the wall in a muddy green. This floor, too, was covered in dark linoleum. The tap dripped into a small sink, behind which bars covered narrow panes that overlooked the same view that had greeted Frances from her own window.

There was little furniture—only a large table covered by a red plush cloth edged with bobbles and surrounded by six dark-stained, battered Windsor chairs, a low cupboard, and a shelf with plain cups and saucers and a silver spirit kettle. Intrigued by a door set in the wall to the left, Frances opened

11

it to see an oak cradle, a crib, and two coffinlike, white-painted iron bedsteads, all with dark blue coverlets. The bareness was relieved by two large pictures in ornate gilt frames, one depicting a bluebell wood in which the trees faded away to gray-lilac recesses and the other of Red Riding Hood being accosted by the wolf. The child's huge eyes and too-yellow curls made her think of Martin Hallowes and his description of the girl his mother expected.

Something ran squeaking into the shadows behind the rigid beds, and her heart fluttered briefly. She didn't mind mice, so long as it had been a mouse. It was strange that the creature had only made its presence known when she'd thought about Lady Hallowes's objectionable son.

A new sound broke into her thoughts, and she quickly turned to leave; she had no desire to be found where she had no right to be. Just in time, Frances emerged into the passage to see a small angular figure toil into sight. This must be Mary, the maid, a poor-looking, plain little girl with lank hair and a drop on the end of her nose that she brushed away with the back of her hand.

"Miss Frances?" she panted, holding her side.

"Yes."

"You're to come to Mrs. Crabbe's room. Now."

"Must it be immediately? Wouldn't you like to get your breath back first?"

Mary stared at her blankly. "Oh, no, miss! She said now."

"I'll say I wasn't quite ready."

"Can't do that, miss. You'd have to tell a lie. But"—the girl's lips trembled into a ghost of a smile—"it was good of you to think of it. Not everyone would."

"You look tired," Frances said, following her.

12

"I get up at five," Mary told her with a certain pride.

"Five! Is that really necessary?"

"There's all the fires to be cleaned and laid and lit and coals brought. It's a fair big house, Hallowes."

"It is. I can't help feeling that's too much for one person so early in the day."

Their footsteps echoed in the confines of the steep staircase. Frances wondered too late if she should be sowing the seeds of rebellion in a girl who obeyed orders so unquestioningly.

"It's summer," she pointed out to the thin figure in the stark uniform that contrasted so pitifully with the romantic trappings Lady Hallowes enjoyed. "Why must there be so many fires anyway?"

"It's a cold building, miss, having such thick walls, and there's things that'd be spoiled if they was to be attacked by damp."

"Things?"

"Pictures, miss, and tapestries. Curtains. Valuables."

"I think people are more important than objects."

"Oh, miss! They be Hallowes treasures!" Mary was visibly shocked. It was plain that she'd been thoroughly indoctrinated into the necessity of the service of Mammon.

"Yes. I suppose they are." Frances thought of her book of pre-Raphaelite prints. Wasn't she just as obsessed by its beauty? Yet there was a difference. She didn't expect anyone to dance attendance upon it, crawling unwillingly from bed in the predawn darkness to warm and cosset it. Was she neglecting it? There was no doubting the fact that she'd made a kind of god of the volume, swearing that if St. Anne's School went on fire, it would be the first thing she'd take to safety.

She was trying to decide whether it was because Papa had given it to her, or if it was for its own haunting charm, when Mary came to a halt in front of another of those perplexing doors and knocked nervously. "It's Miss Frances, Mrs. Crabbe."

"Come in," Aunt Bessie said. "And you can go back to the kitchen, Mary."

The girl scuttled off obediently toward heaven only knew what distasteful task, and Frances made herself enter the small sitting room crowded with ugly furniture, from which as much light as possible was excluded by heavy plush drapes. All of Aunt Bessie's past was in the room. Two pictures of a mutton-chopped Uncle Crabbe in fading sepia. One of Grandfather in the dark shiny suit that seemed his only set of clothes. Another of Grandmother, smiling ever so faintly, in a gown that fastened right under her chin and looked decidedly uncomfortable. Papa in a graduation gown and mortarboard. It was strange to think of her father now dressed in khaki because two foreign aristocrats who must have been total strangers to most of the British had been assassinated in a place called Sarajevo a year ago in 1914, plunging Britain into war with Germany.

Tears swam suddenly in Frances's eyes. She blinked them away resolutely. Papa had his own reasons for enlisting. He wasn't old. He was in perfect health. And he knew how to order people about. There would be no problem getting his job back when he returned as a war hero. He'd smiled rather ironically as he'd said that. General Kitchener wanted all the soldiers he could get.

Frances sat down silently at the supper table. Directly opposite was a huge framed picture of a stag, its feet lost in heather and its antlers outlined against an expanse of cloud that hung over

14

a brooding crag. There was something ridiculous about the whole scene. Slowly, the pain engendered by the memories of Papa was soothed away by the unintentional comedy of the Victorian monstrosity.

She became aware that her aunt was glancing surreptitiously at her hands and her hair.

"Did you hang up your things?"

"Yes. And I put the rest in the drawers."

"Good. There you are. Eat that."

In spite of the fat on the mutton, Frances enjoyed her meal. Mrs. Robertson had made up a parcel of food for the journey, but it had been too dainty and insubstantial for Frances's hearty appetite. Her aunt seemed not disposed to chatter, and that was a relief. As she ate, Frances studied the heavy lines of the walnut worktable in the corner, the central compartment filled with the usual Berlin woolwork bag fringed with tassels. She wondered what Lady Hallowes, with her exquisite taste, would make of it.

"Lady Hallowes says I may explore outside," she said as she finished her rice pudding.

"But on no account must you waste the gardeners' time."

"No, Aunt. Am I allowed to see inside the house?"

"Certain parts only. It's a privilege to be here. I hope you've brought something to do."

"I have to produce an essay about my holiday. And I have books and painting materials."

Aunt Bessie dipped an apostle spoon in the crimped orange-luster sugar bowl she'd had in her own home before she was widowed. The keys at her waist jingled as she leaned forward.

"I'll be able to do any shopping you need, or to exchange your books at the library," offered Frances.

"What should I do with books? Anyway, there's no library."

How empty her life must be, Frances thought with a certain horrified pity.

"I should warn you not to have anything to do with Master Martin. He's a limb of Satan, that boy."

"I doubt if he'll want to bother with me. He pretended he thought I was the kitchen maid."

"Just like him." Aunt Bessie sniffed. "Come to a bad end, I shouldn't wonder."

"Can I help you with the supper things?"

"Someone will collect them. I'm not expected to attend to such matters," Aunt Bessie said grandly.

"I think I'll go for a walk tomorrow. I would like to stretch my legs."

"Remember what I said, Frances. Can you find your way back? I'll come with you and show you the side door. It opens directly onto the servants' stairs. The kitchen is just below that landing. If you are ever in doubt, go down to the kitchen. Never bother any of the family, her ladyship in particular."

"I shan't." Frances imagined that her mention of her own legs was distasteful to her aunt. She probably still approved of valances everywhere and kept the piano legs covered. At school Frances and her friends had giggled wildly when they discovered that gentlemen's trousers were never to be mentioned. But she could never share such a joke with Aunt Bessie. It seemed such a shame.

The lump that had threatened to choke her during the interview with Lady Hallowes became a tight pain in her chest. She'd been able to joke with Papa and some of her school friends. Here there was no one but her aunt and that boy.

"Hasn't she any other children?" Frances asked abruptly.

"Who?"

"Lady Hallowes."

"You must say Lady Hallowes, not she. There was another boy, one of twins. Only Master Martin grew up. Maybe just as well. T'other might have been just as bad."

"Oh, no! He wasn't."

"And how should you know!" Aunt Bessie was displeased.

For the life of her, Frances could never explain why she'd been so sure. It was almost as though that other boy had stood behind her, prompting her in a soft whisper. But she could never tell her aunt any such thing. She'd think her niece was mad, and who would blame her.

"You aren't thinking of going outside tonight, I hope?"

"No, Aunt Bessie. I really feel rather tired. I'll just go to bed."

"Off you go, then. And be careful with the candle."

"Good-night." Frances hesitated for a moment, but her aunt made no attempt to kiss her good-night. She was ashamed of her own relief, but grudging affection was worse than none at all. Briefly, she fancied she heard again that faint, far-off sound of plucked strings. Was it a harp? Lady Hallowes would look very beautiful and romantic seated at a harp, her cloud of dark red hair making shadows against the pale green wall. But there hadn't been a harp in the room.

Aunt Bessie closed her door before she could ask any questions. Frances found the staircase without any trouble, weariness stealing over her like a dusty cloak. Time seemed to stand still. One minute she was downstairs, the next in her bedroom, the candle sending guttering shapes that swooped darkly into corners where they quivered disturbingly.

Frances finished undressing and lay down. There was a faint smell of lavender and wax. The tap still dripped, and each drop

17

of water seemed perfectly spaced out, each sounding like the note of some strange, haunting tune. The faint melody echoed inside her head. She must have that tap seen to tomorrow.

Now that she was in bed she imagined that she'd immediately go to sleep, but she didn't. She lay staring at the wall, conscious of the distant water notes and the moving candle shadows. The wallpaper was decorated with vertical stripes of greenery and small roses. She gazed at the stripes. There was one rose that looked a little like a face, and she studied the pattern in an effort to find one that corresponded. Oddly, there was something magnetic about the thin, flowery stripes. It was almost as though they moved. They *were* moving, and Frances felt her stomach rebel against the sensation that she was falling. Falling very fast, with time rushing past. Time flying and taking her with it. Frances was not sure that she really wanted to go, so she fought against the dizzying motion and the vague roaring that reminded her of a distant train in a long tunnel. She saw a boy's face in the rushing dark. It was Martin Hallowes's face, yet the expression on the features was not his, and neither was the whispering voice that urged, "Come! Please come! Please—"

But she fought too strongly. The face and the feeling of being sucked into space gradually died away, and there was only the dark.

CHAPTER TWO

Hot sunlight blinded her. When her eyes became accustomed to the yellow glare, Frances studied the wallpaper. It looked quite ordinary now, a little faded here and there, with a dampish stain in one corner of the slanting ceiling. The rain had seeped in through faulty lead flashing at one time, and no one had considered the room important enough to redecorate.

But Frances couldn't get the boy's face out of her mind—so like Martin's, yet so unlike. What had he meant by "Come! Please . . . "? Where did he want her to go? The practical side of her nature reasserted itself. She'd been worn out by her long journey, and it had been a little unnerving being in a strange bed so far from the rest of the household. The dripping tap had sounded sinister in the half-dark, bringing a queer life to the deserted nursery rooms. She'd had a nightmare, that was all.

Yet the sound of Mary's boots on the stairs and her knock on the door still made Frances jump. "It's your hot water, miss."

19

"You shouldn't have bothered," Frances said, opening the door. "I could have used the cold in the nursery. I like washing in cold water. It makes you feel fresher."

"Oh, no, miss. You're a guest. Guests are entitled to hot. You'll get breakfast in Mrs. Crabbe's room. She's had hers, o' course. Gets up early, does Mrs. Crabbe. She said to let you sleep late this once."

"I meant to be up long ago. Thank you, Mary."

"That's all right, miss. It's no bother when it's appreciated."

Frances studied the little gold watch pinned to her blouse hanging over the chair. "Great heavens! I must have been more tired than I thought! I'll have to knock my head on the pillow tonight, seven times."

"It's a pretty watch, miss." The girl sounded wistful, though not envious.

"My father gave it to me. A sort of parting present for the duration of the war." Frances felt guilty, sensing that such treasures would never come Mary's way.

"Horrible things, wars, miss," Mary said sympathetically. "You've no other family, have you?"

"Only Aunt Bessie."

"And she won't be any company, being so busy like." Mary echoed Frances's own thoughts. "Sorry, miss. I shouldn't be standing here gossiping."

"You mustn't think I'll mind that. Are you the only maid?"

"Why, no, miss! I'm the scullery maid, but there's parlor, chamber, and house maids. Not all the house is used, o' course. There's not as much money as there used to be. This bit never is, as a rule. Lady Hallowes wasn't sure where to put you, you being—" Mary stopped and went pink with embarrassment.

"Only the housekeeper's niece?" Frances laughed. "Actually, I think I'll enjoy myself. I'm quite fond of my own company. And I'd rather have you than any of the other maids. I think we'll get along very well. You'd better go, though. I can see you chafing at the leash, and I wouldn't want to get you into trouble."

Gratefully, Mary departed, and Frances washed in the big basin with the faint crack in it and the design of blue storks and trees. Something tapped at the window and Frances whirled around, almost expecting to see someone staring through the pane. The skinny fingers of a branch were blown against the glass by a freshening breeze. Looking out, Frances saw that a tree, grown to an immense height, grew to one side of the window. A number of others had also gone to height rather than breadth, but none was as tall as the first. It stood like a sentinel over the gorge below. Frances wondered why this window had no bars like the others, then concluded that this could well have been a nanny or governess's sitting room where the children never came. She thought of the abandoned nursery rooms and of Lady Hallowes's twin sons. How old had Martin's brother been when he died?

With a sense of urgency she began to dry herself, then put on her clothes, her fingers fumbling over the small buttons. Her hair would get short shrift today. Frances took her jacket and purse downstairs with her. It would save time after breakfast, and she had an urge to explore. There was the gorge, and she knew the sea wasn't far away. Plenty of exercise would banish the memory of Papa in his khaki suit and peaked cap, lost in the drifting steam of the departing train.

21

Another girl brought porridge and an egg to Aunt Bessie's sitting room. She was pretty and rather too aware of the fact. Frances gained the impression that she wasn't too pleased to be running about after a guest who wasn't really out of the top drawer. I'm a misfit, Frances thought, seating herself at the little round table. Lady Hallowes doesn't know what to do about me, and neither do the staff. Even Aunt Bessie!

She was surprisingly hungry and ate everything she'd been given. Then she piled the crockery and cutlery neatly on the tray, just as she'd made her own bed so as not to be a trouble to anyone. It seemed little enough to do when so much was being done for her. How was it Martin Hallowes had described her? Lady Hallowes's war work. Salving her conscience. What an unpleasant boy he was!

Dismissing Martin, Frances let herself out by the side door, as Aunt Bessie had instructed her, and sniffed at the morning air, deciding after a struggle between left and right to take the path that looked as though it might go in the direction of the sea. She'd already seen the gorge from her window.

Wild flowers stitched the grassy sides of the track, and she wished she'd brought her sketchbook and paints. Cones had dropped from pines and larch and the dark shadows of yew. Scabious and harebell danced in the shade of lady's bedstraw alongside another yellow plant she didn't recognize. Frances bent to pick a piece. Mary might identify it for her. The scent of clover grew stronger as the sun became lighter and the earth warmed. Clover was lucky if you found any with four leaves. Not many people did. A great beech burned red, fired by the sun's light, and there were yellow leaves left over from autumn, making patterns on the beech mast. But the slender silver of birches predominated, crowding around the sprightly rowans and wild cherry. She'd certainly inherited Papa's love of trees and plants.

The woods began to thin into a straggle of blackberry, bracken, and ancient heather roots. Now the smell of the sea grew tantalizingly strong.

She broke out of the dwindling cover, recognizing the spikes of sedge that fringed the dunes. A track ran, sandy and enticing, through the gap. Frances picked up her skirts and ran in an excess of pleasure toward the pale gray ocean and the solitary stretch of beach. Cumulus clouds piled white and high like woods and palaces of the gods, their remoteness curiously calming and humbling. It seemed impossible, looking out over this serene and lonely place, that Papa was bound for noise and mud, for guns and death. But not his! Frances's breath grew tight in her chest. Other men might die, but not her father. The war had become suddenly and sickeningly real, and though she hadn't cried before, she now wanted to release the pent-up tears.

She discovered, as she fought against the urge, that she was grasping the strange plant almost as though she gained comfort from it.

Something moved in the distance, and she was distracted from her need to sorrow. Staring, she made out a figure on a pony, silhouetted darkly against the sea and sand. As she came closer she saw that the rider was Martin, in gray breeches and black jacket, his face shaded by the brim of a hard hat. He looked older in the riding clothes, with something of his mother's elegance, but his smile was unchanged—sharp and mocking, as though he despised her yet in some odd way enjoyed the encounter.

23

His gaze fell on the yellow plant, and the smile vanished.

"You know what this is?" she asked, and held it toward him so that its dark shadow splotched the pony's side.

Martin backed off a little. "It's St. John's Wort. A protection against witches and evil. If you believe in that sort of thing."

She noticed that he didn't actually go so far as to call it nonsense, as she would have expected. There was something else that disturbed her but that didn't come out into the open, only niggled at the back of her mind like the onset of toothache. She held the plant protectively, thinking that she might press it and put it inside a letter to Papa.

The boy was smiling again, as though he'd sensed her thought and was laughing inwardly at her foolishness.

She never knew what prompted her to ask. "When did your brother die?"

He blinked and shrugged his shoulders as if casting off a burden.

"I'm sorry," she said quickly. "I should have realized—"

"What should you have realized?" he asked.

"That it might be upsetting for you. Your only brother."

"It was a long time ago. Nine years."

"Then he'd be seven or eight?" As you were then, she thought.

"You really want to know, don't you?"

Frances didn't like the way he laughed. "It seems such an awful thing to happen. Like losing half of yourself—"

"That's not the way I looked at it."

She didn't really have the effrontery to ask him how he'd reacted toward his brother's death.

"He was seven," Martin told her, and smiled.

24

Her skin crept. It had not been a sympathetic smile. If she'd had to describe it, she would have labeled it as triumphant. But it wasn't unheard of for brothers to be at loggerheads. Look at Cain and Abel.

Flushing, Frances wondered what had put so awful a thought into her head. It was such an understatement to describe their antipathy in so lukewarm a manner. Only, of course it had been Cain's hatred—Abel had probably been an innocent victim. She wished she could stop thinking about it, but Martin had an aura about him that called up unpleasant things. Her mind always returned to the same adjective to describe the Hallowes boy.

Evil . . .

"If you're so anxious to know about my brother," Martin said nastily, "you can read all the details over there." He pointed his whip toward the distance, beyond the end of the beach where a wall hid most of a small church Frances hadn't previously noticed.

She opened her mouth to say that she wasn't that curious, but he'd already nudged the gray pony to a gallop. It would have been a lie, Frances conceded; she *was* curious, and anyway, he'd ridden off so fast that she wasn't going to demean herself by shouting after him. Perversely, she began to walk away from the churchyard, but it seemed as though her feet were weighted. Each step became more difficult than the last, leaving deep grooves in the damp sand.

She turned her head. Something glittered on top of the church spire, then vanished. Frances turned and began to retrace her steps; now it was quite easy to walk. The edge of the sea slid by in loops of gray, shifting lace, first spilled then sucked back by the pull of the tide. The moon was supposed

25

to influence the sea, though this wasn't one of the days when its pale ghost haunted the sky. She must look for it tonight from her high window.

The church spire grew nearer, and she could make out a gilded weathercock and patterns of orange lichen on the wall; then there were the slanting shadows of a black ironwork gate. It creaked as Frances unlatched it, as if few people ever used it. Old gravestones leaned, tired of the weight of past centuries.

There was one that was grander than the rest, a tall stone inside railings that surrounded a widish plot that must contain several graves. She leaned on the black-painted rail, looking for the most recent grave, and found it almost immediately. A small white stone bore the legend:

IN LOVING MEMORY OF

SIMON,

SON OF RICHARD AND JANE HALLOWES,

DROWNED, AGED SEVEN YEARS.

Drowned? How? And where? Frances guessed that Martin had sent her here deliberately, knowing that she'd come away little wiser. She stared at the white marble, aware of a feeling of unhappiness she found hard to explain. It was almost as if she'd been summoned to mourn for a child she had never seen. If he'd lived, would he have been like his twin?

The grasses shook suddenly and violently, and the weathercock on the steeple spun crazily, then slowly stilled, pointing in another direction. Her eyes followed the line indicated, and she saw another thin path entering the trees. Though she had planned to walk back along the beach, she

26

felt a compulsion to go into the wood in search of whatever was concealed there.

As she passed the tall stone in the center of the plot, the names of dead Halloweses leaped out at her. Richard, Martin, Simon, and was that Francesca? The carving of the woman's name was obviously older than the rest, and the chiseling had lost its sharpness long ago. Peering, Frances decided that she'd been right. There'd been an Elizabeth and an Agnes and a pathetic little Margaret, who'd lived for only two months.

Even more ancient stones leaned against the railings at the back of the plot, overshadowed by the central stone that rose far above the others. Black yews pressed close to the barrier, casting a threatening shade.

Another gate led out of the churchyard. It was not so much in need of oiling as the one on the seaward side, and this path led directly toward the woodland track she'd glimpsed over the wall. Nettles stung her through her clothing as she plunged into the cold, green depths. Dots of itchy fire made her shiver and long to scratch her skin. Here there was no sunlight shining on pretty wildflowers and airy trees. There was something in this wood that reminded her of Grimms' fairy tales and the pages of Hans Christian Andersen—a sour smell of decay and fungus instead of the warm pleasant perfumes of clover and resin. Sharp twigs snatched at her legs and pulled threads in her skirt. Frances repressed the exclamation that rose to her lips. She'd been foolish to come into this plantation, where everything pressed closer and closer together as though it sought to imprison her.

Only a small vestige of sky could be seen here and there. Something crackled close-by. Frances stood perfectly still.

27

There was only the sound of her own breathing and a tiny sough of wind. Then she had the terrible fancy that hers was not the only noise of breathing.

She clenched her hands, forcing herself to think that other villagers must use the wood and the surroundings of Hallowes. In spite of the gloom, it was daylight. The path had vanished, so she pushed her way toward the greatest area of light. Slowly the wood opened out again. Trees had been cut down at some time here, and the flat stumps remained, coated with spongy moss.

Something on the ground gleamed dully as she kicked aside a covering of decomposed leaves and rotted twigs, revealing a broken leather box. Bending down, Frances saw that it contained a ring with a large oval stone. Rubbing away the encrusted mud, she saw that the stone appeared to be a huge opal, and that the thick silver shanks of the setting were chased into a pattern of twigs and leaves. Even in the dimness, the stone gave off iridescent glints of red, green, and blue. It did not matter which way she held the ring; it always contained some lifelike scene or other. A red desert rippled under a blue and purple sky. Sunset glowed over a peacock sea. Red water plunged through a gap between seamed cliffs. An underground river forced its way between the carved walls of a vast cave. Frances found herself being drawn toward the undulating folds of the desert where purple shadows lay in the dunes.

The sensation was so strong that Frances was only half-aware of a familiar voice calling, "Miss Frances? Is that you?" A thin figure pushed aside the bushes.

Frances returned to earth with a jolt. "Mary?"

"Yes, miss. It's Mary. It's near lunchtime, and Mrs. Crabbe wants you to come."

Frances dropped the ring into her pocket. "It can't be that time already?" She frowned, thinking that time had indeed flown. And yet, in another way, the morning seemed to have lasted forever. She forgot the ring in her anxiety not to displease her aunt. "But how did you know where I was?"

"Master Martin said you were at the church and reminded your aunt that this is the quickest way home."

Master Martin was a real know-it-all, Frances thought, and wished she could overcome her dislike. Then she put all her mind to following Mary back to the house.

CHAPTER THREE

Aunt Bessie sent Frances to the village in the afternoon to collect Lady Hallowes's tonic from the pharmacy. "It's little enough to do for her ladyship."

"Yes, Aunt." Frances was aware that she was in disfavor for returning with threads caught in her navy skirt and green stains from the moss, not to mention her mud-stained hands. She'd been sent upstairs to wash and to brush her hair. After tea, she was to pull the threads to the back of the navy serge.

"And don't come back looking so like a hoyden."

"No, Aunt."

Frances started off down the long drive, remembering too late that she hadn't said anything about her find. It was a pity that Mary had come just at that moment. She should have unearthed the rest of the small box, which had obviously been buried long ago and disintegrated because of the rain and weather. It was curious that she'd had such a prolonged lapse of memory, especially after such an exciting discovery.

She slid her hand into her pocket. The ring was still

there, hard and knobbly, the smooth surface of the stone icy cold. Her fingertips tingled. Closing her eyes, she could see the red desert under the parrot sky, the sunset sea, and the river in the cave.

Even when she removed her hand she could recall the pictures in the opal. The real world, in contrast, looked far less colorful, and the drive was longer than she'd remembered. She'd been told to turn right at the bottom to reach the village.

Halfway down the drive, she could look down into the gorge from a sturdy stone bridge. There was a sign on the bank below, beside a black pool, that said: DANGER. DEEP WATER. The water did indeed look bottomless, the dark surface glittering wickedly in what little light penetrated the thick bushes and overgrowing trees. Beyond the pool, the river sounded turbulent, threatening her with punishment if she should dare to come too close. She seemed, suddenly, to have been at Hallowes for a very long time. Her old home had receded into the distance, and Papa's features were difficult to imagine.

"Don't let me forget him!" she cried out, then chided herself for her foolishness. But Hallowes had turned out to be such an odd, scary place, with its dripping taps, old wallpaper, tapping branches, and haunted churchyards. Where better to find ghosts? Ghosts!

Frances laughed and made herself turn very resolutely at the drive's end toward the scatter of distant cottages. The sun was hot now, and she was glad of her straw boater with the navy band. The woven basket Aunt Bessie had given her was light, and she swung it as she walked. Now that she was close to it, she looked forward to acquainting herself with the village. Each new place was an adventure.

The smell of salt grew stronger, and as she turned a bend

in the road she saw the sea again, lapping almost to the house fronts, yet kept in its place by a narrow stone promenade. So Hallowes must stand on a kind of peninsula, and the railway station where she'd arrived must be positioned higher up the hill, with the trees and houses shutting out a view of the waterfront.

She stopped to look at a cluster of odd-looking basket affairs on the pebbles.

"Lobster pots," a voice said behind her, and she turned to see Martin Hallowes emerge from a small, dark, shop doorway, carrying a parcel.

"I hadn't seen one before." Frances waited for him to go, but he didn't move. The silence grew heavy before he said, "Did you find what you wanted?"

"I found what you wished me to find."

"How very mysterious! Quite cryptic," he mocked.

Frances remembered that she'd discovered more than the burial plot, but some perverse caution made her keep the finding of the ring to herself.

Martin frowned. "What did you do with the St. John's Wort?"

She tried to remember, but there was a blank between recalling having it at the graves and the appearance of Mary. She must have put it down when she knelt to pick up the ring. Yes, that was right! That was what she'd done.

"So you *were* in the south wood," the boy said, almost accusingly. Once again he had read her thoughts.

"Mary said it was a shortcut to Hallowes, as well you know."

"That was where you left it," he murmured, apparently

to himself. "I wonder why?" And he shot her a look that was unfriendly.

"I was being attacked by brambles. Look at my skirt."

"Yes. It's a pig of a wood. No one much goes there."

"Not even the churchgoers?"

"They stick to the north wood. There's a better path only a few feet away, if only you'd looked further."

"You forget, I'm a stranger."

"Of course. I should choose the north wood next time." It sounded like a threat.

"Thank you for your concern."

Martin smiled. "That sounds almost insulting."

"Do you think so?"

"It's all right. I won't tell Mama."

Frances flushed. "There's nothing to tell."

"What are you doing here, anyway?"

"Looking for the pharmacist's shop."

"Ah, Mama's medicine. Your chore for today. You aren't allowed to be let scot-free. Wouldn't you rather have been doing something else?"

"Not at all. I'll enjoy getting to know the village." Frances wanted to ask him why he couldn't have collected his mother's prescription but thought better of it and turned on her heel. She thought she heard Martin laugh as she walked away, but she couldn't be sure. Her cheeks still burned.

The smell of the tangle rose, rank and strong. A small boat maneuvered itself inside the breakwater. Gulls settled expectantly. Frances decided she'd walk back on the shingle like a beachcomber.

There was a jangling bell in the pharmacist's shop. Light

33

shone through the three huge bottles of colored water that stood in the window. Red, blue, and green, like the gaudy colors in the ring. She stared, mesmerized.

"Yes, miss?" The voice was impatient, as though its owner had already spoken. A small, bearded man was at the counter.

"Oh! I'm sorry. I've come for Lady Hallowes's medicine."

"Lady Hallowes, eh?" The old man was mollified. "Aye, it's all ready." He opened a door in the glass-fronted cupboard behind him and took out a sealed paper parcel.

Frances thanked him and put it carefully into the basket. "Aren't they beautiful?" she said. "Those huge bottles in the window."

"Hmm. I suppose they are. It's a long time since I really looked at them. Visiting Hallowes, are you?"

"For the summer."

"I wish you joy of your stay."

"Thank you."

"A relative of the family, are you? I hadn't heard of any girl cousins, not of your age."

"I'm Mrs. Crabbe's niece. Lady Hallowes has been very kind in allowing me to stay for some weeks."

"Hmm," the old man mused. "I wouldn't have thought . . .," and his voice trailed away.

Frances waited for the old man to complete the sentence, but he didn't.

"That was Lady Hallowes's son who just went by," she remarked, wanting to know more about Martin.

The old man grunted. "Don't see much of that one. Young Simon was a different kettle of fish." His old voice softened. "You'd never have found a nicer lad if you'd searched the wide world. Always a smile, and something in his voice

34

that made you feel somehow—as if you mattered. There's no one round these parts who knew Simon Hallowes who's forgotten him. Changed his mother, that boy's death did. She kept open house before she lost him. That's why it seemed strange she'd—" Again he regained sufficient caution not to say what he was thinking of Frances's presence.

"Good day," Frances said.

"Daresay we'll be seeing you again."

"I daresay." The bell clanged again as she opened the door, letting in a transient flow of brightness; then it stopped as she closed the door behind her.

She wondered, as she moved on, why Lady Hallowes had done something that was so out of character. Her self-questioning did not last long. There were more immediate interests: the cramped grocer's shop, from which the evocative smells of ground coffee and bacon emerged, and a dear little bow-fronted confectioner's called Peggy's, which displayed a selection of homemade humbugs, boxes of fudge, tablet, treacle toffee, little brown sticks of locust, wads of Spanish, very black and difficult to chew, and tins of toffees.

Peggy, if indeed it were she, turned out to be a wizened little woman, very sharp and bright of eye, who looked hard at Frances and seemed to have difficulty with her English accent, while her own was almost unintelligible to her bemused customer. However, by dint of perseverance and much pointing, Frances obtained a box of fudge for Lady Hallowes, treacle toffee for her aunt, a tin of humbugs for Mary, a piece of Spanish for herself because it was so long lasting, and some locust because she liked it so much.

Outside, her basket heavier now, Frances hurried past a small butcher's establishment, the sides of meat and poultry hanging up on hooks and the flies buzzing, and a cottage with its door open to reveal an assortment of vegetables, a barrel of potatoes, and a box of wrinkled apples.

Beyond this point there were only low dwellings crouched over small strips of ground on which vegetables and fruit trees grew and a few goats and cows were tethered.

Having exhausted the possibilities of the hamlet, she made her way down some steps and onto the pebbly shore, her boots crunching on the pale, smooth stones, her hair whisked back by a freshening breeze. Gulls made white arcs in the sky, and a collie ran down to the surf, barking with pleasure until he was recalled by a burly, bad-tempered man in rough clothing, a gray plaid over one shoulder. He brandished a crook, obviously grudging the dog its short-lived joy in living.

The road seemed longer than ever, being all uphill. Here and there hoofmarks showed on the ground, and Frances was reminded of Martin and the ring. She decided that once the medicine was delivered, she would return to the south wood to examine the remains of the box. Again she slid her hand into her pocket and felt for the ring. It was still there, cold and curiously heavy. She let go of it with a kind of revulsion.

The house came into sight quite suddenly, shocking her into momentary stillness by the force of its magnetism. She almost went up to the front steps, then remembered that housekeepers' nieces had to use side doors.

It was cold going around the corner, and she shivered as she let herself in. Remembering the object of her journey, she went down the stairs that led to the kitchen. A baize-covered door greeted her. She knocked and heard Aunt Bessie shouting, "Who is it?"

"Frances."

"Come in, then." Aunt Bessie sounded harassed.

Frances had to push very hard, as the door was on a heavy spring. The green baize felt sandpapery and odd to the touch after the customary smoothness of paint. It closed after her with a dull thud.

"I didn't know what to do with the medicine."

"Oh, that. I'll take charge of it."

Handing over the wrapped bottle, Frances stared at the immensity of the kitchen with its huge gray flagstones and big, black-leaded Cannon range on which a variety of copper pans and kettles rested. There was one like it in her own home, but only a third the size. A bread oven gaped out of the wall beside it, and something on a spit turned in front of an open fire in the corner.

Mary, busy at a large double sink, smiled and went on with her washing up, stacking the dishes and ashets in a big wooden rack on the wall.

"I got this," Frances said awkwardly, taking out the box of fudge. "For her ladyship for having me."

Aunt Bessie grunted approvingly, her heavy-lidded, rather protuberant eyes resting on the other packages in the basket.

"This one's for you."

"Thank you, child. I'll see that Lady Hallowes gets hers."

Copper jelly molds and a brass jam pan winked on a shelf above an array of blue-and-white china. The smell of the roast was inviting.

"May I leave the basket here just now? I'd like to go out again for a little."

"So long as you're back in an hour to clean up. And mind your skirt."

37

"Yes, Aunt."

The baize door was just as hard to open from this side, but Frances supposed it had to fit tightly to keep in all the smells of cooking and the steam they wouldn't want to filter upstairs to spoil the curtains and pictures.

Once outside, she found it easy to retrace her steps toward the tangled path of the south wood. A few more pulled threads wouldn't be noticed, and she was going to have to repair the damage tonight so the visit couldn't be left until tomorrow.

Frances edged her way there carefully, moving toward the greatest area of light, which obviously was where the trees had been cut down. She emerged, relieved, by the ring of green stumps and hurried around them, her eyes searching the earth for the place where the rotted box had been uncovered. The yellow flowers on the spray of St. John's Wort glimmered against the leaf mold, and she almost ran toward it, then stood still, staring at the disturbed ground.

The box was gone.

CHAPTER FOUR

Disturbed by the removal of the box, Frances picked up the yellow flowers and returned to the house for her meal and to repair the damage to her skirt. She blamed Martin for taking away the remains of the little box, yet how could she be sure? Just because he'd noticed the absence of the plant wasn't proof, but her instincts told her that he'd wanted to know where she'd abandoned the flowers. The only other person who knew where she'd been was poor, honest Mary. Then Frances remembered the moment when she'd been convinced that there was someone else in the darkness of the wood, that someone else was breathing close-by, and she shivered.

Her aunt was in a tetchy mood, and Frances found it difficult to make conversation over their joyless supper, barely noticing what they ate and drank.

"I'll give you the needles and thread," Aunt Bessie said as soon as they'd finished. "You can do your sewing here."

"Oh, there's much more light upstairs," Frances said

quickly, looking at the heavy, obscuring curtains. "It won't be easy seeing those pulled threads."

"I thought you'd have had more sense at your age," her aunt remarked tartly. "A great girl of nearly fifteen. Skirts don't grow on trees."

Frances said nothing.

"Sulking, are we? Well, you'd best take it upstairs then."

"Very well."

"Mary will fetch up your hot water."

It was on the tip of Frances's tongue to protest, and then she thought how pleasant it would be to talk to Mary, even if it was only for a few minutes.

"Perhaps she'd bring my basket from the kitchen at the same time. I forgot to go back for it. It's not in the least heavy." It seemed the perfect opportunity to give Mary her gift.

Aunt Bessie grunted and opened a drawer to look for the mending box.

Once upstairs, Frances felt wrapped in an intense loneliness, broken only by the dripping of the tap. She tried closing the door of the nursery, but that seemed even worse, almost as though she'd shut out someone she loved. The falling drops began to form the ancient music that had haunted her last night. *Drop, drop, drop, splash. Drop, drop, drop, splash.* Like the first eerie waltz, long before Strauss.

Sighing, she picked up her sewing, aware now of another sound, that of the thin branches of the great tree tapping at the small window like skeletal fingers.

Pushing away that unpleasant fancy, she began to sew. By the time she'd finished the exacting task, the light had started to go, and her eyes ached. Feeling in her pocket for her handkerchief, she again touched the ring. She should have

40

told Aunt Bessie she'd found it. Why hadn't she? How could the finding of so exciting an object keep slipping from her mind? It seemed almost as though she wasn't intended to tell anyone. Then she told herself that inanimate objects couldn't influence people's minds, and it was going to be very awkward, indeed, to bring up the subject of the ring after this time lapse. She'd be expected to say where it was found, and her aunt would know how long ago that was, after the business of her damaged skirt. However much Frances hated lying, she saw she might have to or remain in perpetual disgrace, and it was bad enough having Papa away at the war without incurring Aunt Bessie's eternal disapproval.

Frances was thinking how odd it was for someone to go around burying jewelry when the branches tapped again, and she went to the window to stare at a gun-metal gray sky and an enormous pale moon that hung behind the blackly etched twigs that scratched for admittance.

Moonbranches, she thought. Moonbranches, and the words merged with the notes of water music.

She was subtly aware of other presences, shadows shifting over the mistletoe moon, Simon Hallowes's whispery voice saying, "Help me. Help me. It will be easier for you now. Don't forget me."

Frances thought of the old man in the pharmacist's shop. People didn't forget Simon. She wished she'd known him. And even more, she wanted to know why he continued to seek her out.

Someone knocked at the door. Frances turned to face the room. She seemed to have been away for a very long time, caught on the fringes of another, much older world where sights and smells, textures and sounds were definably older.

41

Her skin retained the sensation of having worn strange material, and she knew that her hair had been long enough to brush her forearm. There'd been a spicy aroma that covered something far less pleasant, and dust had pricked at her nose.

"Miss Frances?"

Frances let go of the world behind the thin curtain of past senses, feeling a little faint and drained of all energy.

"Mary, please come in."

The door opened. "Why, you're in the dark!" Mary exclaimed, setting down the brass hot-water can and basket and going for the strike-light to light the candle, then the oil lamp. By its calm, yellow glow she studied Frances's pale face. "You look tuckered out, miss."

"I am rather tired."

"There's your basket."

"Oh, yes. The basket. I wanted something from it." She took out the tin with the pictures of King George and Queen Mary on one side and Sandringham Towers on the other. "It's just a few sweets."

"Oh, miss. Them pictures are lovely. Ever such a nice face he has, and as for her, every inch a queen. Shall I open it? Give you one now?"

"Not till you want to. Have you any other chores tonight?"

"No, miss. I was on my way to bed."

"Spare me a few more minutes while I wash. Have a piece of locust. I've got plenty. Thanks for the hot water and lighting the lamp. I—I was looking out of the window at the moon and forgot the time."

"Ever so queer you looked for a moment." Mary inspected

42

the piece of locust. "Almost like—someone else. 'Twould be a trick of the light."

"How did I look?" Frances set down the can beside the blue-and-white basin and began to unbutton her blouse.

"Your hair looked that long, and I thought you had a white dress with little holes in it—"

"Broderie anglaise."

"What?"

"English embroidery. In French."

"Seems a bit silly." Mary laughed. "But it's real clever of you knowing another language. English embroidery in French! Whatever next! But it's not as daft as thinking I saw you in something you aren't wearing, and with your hair down to your waist. Shadowy old places, these rooms. You can't help feeling that there's something left behind, some part of all those children who spent their days in the nursery."

"*All* those children?" Frances wet her face and neck.

"Oh, I don't mean just the twins. There must have been others before them, and before them."

"Did you know Simon Hallowes?"

"Oh, no, miss. That happened before we come here." Frances picked up the towel and dabbed at her skin. "That?"

"The drowning. In that deep pool under the bridge."

Frances drew in her breath sharply. "The one halfway down the drive?"

"That's it, Miss Frances."

Frances's mind struggled with the image of a small boy thrashing about in that blackness, his mouth a round O. Screaming—all to no avail.

43

"Couldn't he swim?" She could almost feel his terror and despair.

"No, miss."

"And wasn't anyone else there?"

"Only Master Martin. He tried to push out a stick, but little Simon couldn't get hold of it. So then he ran to the stables for help, but you know how far away that is. When they got back there, it was too late."

"Poor little boy." Mechanically, Frances hung up the towel and picked up her hairbrush.

"Would you like me to brush your hair, miss? That's what I really fancy, being a lady's maid. Please let me."

"Very well." In truth, Frances was glad to sit down. She felt as if she'd run a very long way and that her legs wouldn't carry her as far as the bed. "Lady Hallowes—and her husband, of course—must have been very upset."

"Oh, they were, especially with Master Simon being the heir and brought up to believe he'd be Master of Hallowes."

"But I thought—"

"Even with twins there's always one born first."

"Of course. How stupid of me."

"Townsfolk doesn't have much to do with birthing. Not like country people. You weren't to know that."

"No. Even if I'd had a mother, I doubt if she'd have explained such things to me. If I had a daughter, I'd think she ought to be better informed. At the proper time."

"Am I doing this right, miss?"

Mary's touch on the hairbrush was firm yet gentle, and Frances was soothed. "Just right."

"It was ever so good of you to give me the tin of sweets."

"It's little enough for all the trotting about you're doing

on my behalf. What's that pretty girl called? The one who brought my breakfast."

"She is bonny," Mary agreed wistfully. "Jenny."

"Handsome is as handsome does," Frances told her. "I'd rather have you any day."

"I'd better go now, though. My room's next to the others, and they'll soon notice if I'm not there. And I do have to be up early."

"Of course. My hair feels lovely. Will you do it every night?"

"Oh, yes, miss." Mary put down the brush and picked up the painted tin she so obviously treasured. "Good-night."

"Good-night, Mary."

It was quiet after she'd gone. The moon was larger and brighter than ever behind the interlacing branches, and the drops from the tap sounded clearly though her door was shut.

Too weary to do more than to struggle out of her clothes and slip her nightgown over her head, Frances turned out the lamp and got into bed. For a second, before she snuffed out the candle on her bedside table, she thought she saw the pattern on the wallpaper move. Then she was lying between the cool sheets, her eyes closed and only a very faint roaring in her ears, the sort of sound that a distant waterfall might make. Soon she was carried away on a dark tide of sleep.

CHAPTER FIVE

"Lady Hallowes would like to see you before you go out,"
Aunt Bessie said when Frances appeared, rather pale and list-
less, for breakfast. "I'll take you along to the right door. And
what's the matter with you?"

"I just feel rather tired. I dreamed a lot."

They'd been jumbled dreams, and Frances hadn't been
herself. She'd been a shadowy stranger with long, dark hair
and a dress that came to just above her ankles, calling out to
Simon in a variety of only half-seen places and clutching
uselessly at the dark.

Then the dark had turned to light, and she was in the
drawing room at Hallowes. Though most of the faces that
surrounded her were those of strangers, she saw Sir Richard
and Lady Hallowes standing by the white marble fireplace
where the flames burned red and gold, warming the cold,
gleaming stone.

Staring downward, Frances saw that she was wearing a white dress that was not her own. It fit her perfectly, though, creamy white, with the little holes around the hem carefully embroidered with ivory silk. She touched the folds of the skirt, and now it felt familiar.

She looked around the room, where everyone was either dancing or talking in the corners. Above her head the heavy droplets of a chandelier glittered, sending out sharp facets of rich color: scarlet, emerald, and blue. The sound of the music took hold of her senses so that she longed to become involved in the dance.

Pleasure left her sharply. Martin was there on the staircase that overlooked the large room. Dressed all in black, he seemed to cast a shadow over the entire proceedings, like a bird of prey over a nest of field mice.

Frances shivered. Someone touched her lightly. "May I have the pleasure of this dance?" Though Martin hadn't moved he seemed to be standing in front of her now, but his aura was very different. "Martin?" she said, puzzled.

"No, Simon. It's Simon. Please let's dance." Then they were moving together in the steps of the waltz, and Simon Hallowes was holding her around the waist, the warmth of his arm curiously comforting and right, as though he'd done the same thing many times before and would do so again.

"Of course. Simon. How could I have thought you were he?" and she stared up at the staircase but Martin had gone, taking away the portent of doom. She closed her eyes, completely wrapped up in the sensation of safety and belonging, of the unfolding of a happiness that lay only with the tall, young boy who took such obvious pleasure in her company.

She smiled. Then the music became strange and jangled and made the cold pieces of the chandelier strike one another like weapons. The room became icy.

"Help me," Simon cried out, his voice despairing, and Frances tried to hold him to her, but something dark and wicked had entered the dream that was stronger than either of them. Simon was gone and Martin had taken his place.

Together they circled the floor, the music becoming more and more distorted and the room more and more frozen and shadow-filled. Then she'd jerked out of sleep to a feeling of loss and deprivation that had cast a gloom over her spirits.

"Nightmares by the look of you. Just keep out of them woods, that's all. Nasty, dangerous places for all they're so close to the church." Aunt Bessie surveyed Frances's skirt with a critical eye, but finding nothing to complain about, she poured her niece a cup of tea and passed it across the comfortably laden table.

All the way through breakfast Frances wondered why Lady Hallowes should wish to talk to her. After all, she'd been doing what was expected of her and had kept out of everyone's way. Perhaps Martin had reported the gist of their last conversation. He'd said that he wouldn't, but she could never trust someone as unpredictable as Martin. She thought of the way he'd invaded her dream and hated him for spoiling what had been so agreeable.

"Better see her ladyship now, and whatever you do after that, keep out of mischief and be back by twelve."

Being in Aunt Bessie's care was like having a nanny, Frances thought, but it wouldn't be forever. Just this summer, then everything would go back to normal. It would, wouldn't it? Her own doubts took the form of a dull pain in her chest.

"Whatever are you looking like that for?" her aunt cried. "She's not going to have you put in the stocks or hanged on the village green."

"I suppose not." Frances was cheered by this unexpected flash of humor, black though it was. Perhaps there was another side to this formidable woman. Then, following the small, stout figure along the confusing passages, her heart sank again and she wished herself miles away.

Lady Hallowes's voice replied softly to Aunt Bessie's firm knock. "Who is that?"

"I brought Frances as you asked, Lady Hallowes."

"Oh, yes. Do come in, child."

Frances stepped into the room. Today there was less light to fall through the loops of heavy lace, and the glass dome glimmered icily. Even the branch, the grasses, and the long-dead flowers inside it seemed touched with thin frost. The gray-green walls reminded her of mistletoe berries. Even the touches of rust red on the Chinese jars and in the carpet didn't take away from the chilliness of the effect.

Today Martin's mother was wearing a dress only a shade darker than the wallpaper, which had a silky sheen and looked very rich in spite of its pale neutrality. It wasn't the sort of room into which one could introduce a dog, a cat, or rackety children.

"I wanted to thank you for your kind thought."

Kind thought? Frances frowned.

"The sweets are my husband's favorite."

"Oh, those." Frances reddened. "I just saw them when I went to the village."

"Nevertheless, it was thoughtful. But we wouldn't like

you to spend too much of your allowance on us, much though we appreciate it."

"I couldn't stay without doing something. I did think of flowers but nobody was selling those."

Lady Hallowes sat down on her pale sofa and invited her guest to do the same. Frances began to wonder what her husband looked like.

"Are you managing to occupy yourself?"

"Oh, yes. I like to explore new places, and I've brought my painting and sketching things."

The beautiful face lit up briefly. "You enjoy art?"

"I'm not very good at it, but I do enjoy it."

"Then you must go into the gardens if it's fine. You'll find flowers there. I'll tell Angus and Neil that you have permission. I did wonder—"

"Yes, your ladyship?"

"Whether you are finding it too—quiet up in the nursery quarters?"

"No, Lady Hallowes. There's a dripping tap, but apart from that it's very nice."

"You don't find it too lonely?"

Frances shook her head.

"Well, if you get bored, or if the weather's too bad to go out, I believe there are some things in the attic that might amuse you. Mary can show you how to get in."

"Thank you, your ladyship."

Feeling that she was being politely dismissed, Frances stood up again. "If you need your medicine collected again, your ladyship, I'd be happy to get it for you."

"Thank you, my dear." Lady Hallowes rose gracefully, looking quite pleased. "I'm so glad you are fitting in so well.

50

One can't know in advance how a situation will turn out, but this one shows that my intuition was right. Martin says he's seen you in the vicinity of the church."

"Yes, he did. I walked through the graveyard."

Lady Hallowes's face changed. "Then you must have seen my poor darling's stone. I often picture him there, looking the image of Martin. They were identical twins. Yet for all that, very few people mistook one for the other. I never quite understood it."

Frances had the absolute conviction that she did. "It was very sad. I'm so sorry," she replied conventionally.

"But there you are. No one can change it." Lady Hallowes sighed.

"There was another stone, a very old one. It had the name Francesca on it, but I couldn't read the date or anything else."

"My husband would know all about it. It would be some ancestor or other. He delights in digging up the past." Lady Hallowes dismissed the subject. "Well, my dear, you don't want to waste your morning. Try the roses. They are very fine this year, and some of the shrubs are a delight."

"Thank you."

Once outside the too-perfect room, Frances returned to reality. The passage looked reassuringly normal. She began to look forward to seeing the garden. Then thoughts of Simon and the mysterious Francesca intruded, reminding Frances of the strangeness of Hallowes. It was not only Lady Hallowes's room that was odd and filled with portents. There was also the nursery.

Finding her way back to the servants' stairs without too much difficulty—she had memorized the position of a suit of armor and a circular pattern of swords and targes arranged on the wall—Frances began to climb the steps toward her room.

Remembering the ring, she realized that she could have told Lady Hallowes about finding it in the wood. She felt in her pocket to reassure herself that it was still there, and was reminded that she'd taken it out before starting to mend her skirt; she had put it in her handkerchief and stocking drawer.

There were footsteps on the stairs above and the sound of someone whistling a few bars of "The Eriskay Love Lilt." Frances loved this old Scots song. A long shadow tilted over the treads and Martin came into view. He stopped when he saw Frances, laughing at her look of surprise.

"It *is* my house," he said, with that uncanny knack of reading her thoughts exactly.

"Of course."

"I was looking for you, as a matter of fact."

"Oh, why?"

"There was an article in the paper about the state of the war. I thought you'd be interested."

Something in his expression told her that the news would be bad. Even worse was the conviction that he'd enjoy her distress. "How very kind of you."

"Isn't it," he agreed. "By the way, I won't be here all week. I've been invited to stay with a friend. Will you miss me?"

"Why ever should I?" Try though she would, she couldn't keep the hostility out of her voice.

"Oh, well, at least you didn't say you wouldn't. That would have been very bad manners, wouldn't it, and you are so well brought up! Yes and no to your aunt when she requires it, thank you to Mama and offerings of sweetmeats. Fetching her medicine like some little lap dog."

"Must you always try to hurt?"

"Should the truth hurt?" he mocked. "It is true, after all."

"Very well, I'll be very glad indeed that I needn't see you for a week! I wish it could be longer."

He smiled then, and his face was flushed with a sort of triumph.

"And you are welcome to tell your parents what I said. I doubt if they'll believe you," she said hotly, and pushed past him to continue her way upstairs, aware that he watched her until the angle of the staircase shut her from view. The sound of his whistling followed her, and she thought she would never enjoy that tune again, for Martin Hallowes had spoiled it for her. When she reached her room the feeling of peace she usually experienced was replaced by anger that he'd been there.

The newspaper lay on the table and she seized it, reading the dark stories of battle and setbacks, of heroism and the mounting reports of death and names of missing soldiers. She wanted to cry out, but her pride wouldn't allow it. Papa couldn't be there yet. He'd still be safe. But for how long? Why had he gone?

She sat there for a time, her heart aching. Then she reproved herself for her lack of faith. She would write to her father this evening and enclose the piece of St. John's Wort. Last night she'd put it under a loose corner of the linoleum and set a chair over it to press it. Perhaps she hadn't left it long enough to dry properly, but if it should possess the magic properties Martin had mentioned, Papa must have it as quickly as possible. She'd tell him to keep it in his breast pocket. Arms and legs could be repaired. Hearts couldn't.

Thinking of the yellow flowers made her walk to the chest of drawers to take a look at the ring. She felt in the corner under her best handkerchief, but there was nothing there. A fragrance stole out of the drawer. The linings were often made of cedar. The things in the drawer didn't look as tidy as she'd left them. Someone had searched her room.

Martin had looked so pleased with himself. It must have been Martin. But through the anger she felt, Frances was also aware of a sense of relief. She was absolved from the need to mention the ring. Then she thought of what mischief Martin might cause by telling his parents that she'd found it and had said nothing, and her relief turned to misery. Still, there was such a thing as a treasure trove. Remembering that she'd had no intention to steal, she felt better.

Frances seized her painting things, knowing that it was best to try to occupy her mind now. Painting had always soothed her in times of stress. She stopped at the kitchen to ask for an old jar, and Mary told her that there was a pump outside, so she wouldn't need to carry the water too far.

It wasn't too difficult to find the flower gardens, which were enclosed inside a high wall to protect them from the wind. Rock plants and hardier shrubs grew in rocky terraces halfway down the gorge. She was in a mood for the tranquility of flowers, so she opened the gate in the wall and emerged into a world of brilliance and warmth, of scents and droning bees.

Setting down her case of paints, she went to the pump for her jar of water and returned. There were wooden seats

54

placed at intervals, and she chose one near the roses, which, as Lady Hallowes had promised, were at their best. One, a dark bluish red with tightly whorled petals that reminded her of miniature cabbages, attracted her as much by its fragrance as by its appearance. Setting out her paintbox, she chose a brush and began to stroke in the background. The sun, trapped between the high walls, was warm enough to dry the mixture of mysterious greens and grays, so that she could begin the flowers themselves. Her fingers seemed to move of their own volition, almost as if she'd done this many times before. The first rose stared up at her from the paper, complete and perfect, unlike anything she'd ever painted before. She started on the next, and the next.

It was some time before she noticed the shadow that lay long and black over the gravel. Frances became very still.

"Do go on," a man's voice told her. "You mustn't let me put you off. That's very good. I suppose you must be Frances. My wife told me you might be here."

Sir Richard was tall and pleasant faced, not in the least like his son. But Martin, of course, favored his beautiful mother, as had Simon.

The rose leaves shivered suddenly, and Frances realized how long she'd been there at her self-appointed task. "I can easily move if you wish to have the garden to yourself," she said. "I must have been here for ages."

"You certainly are dedicated. I could see you from my window and I confess to having been curious. I'm quite taken with your pictures. Oddly enough, they remind me of some very old sketches by an ancestress of mine who lived here when the house was new. That was in the eighteenth century. I have the sketches in my study. There's one of that same rose you picked. If I put them together I doubt if you'd know the difference."

"I'm sure you're just being kind. Oh, dear, I shouldn't have said that, should I?"

Sir Richard sat down at the other end of the bench and looked at his crossed feet. "My dear, let me say that I find it refreshing that you should be so honest. Some can be so—devious. Only you're wrong. I meant every word of my praise. I must show you poor Francesca's work—"

"Francesca!"

"You've heard of her?" Sir Richard's kind face was puzzled.

"I saw her gravestone. Only her name." Frances wondered why he'd said poor Francesca. "Lady Hallowes didn't seem to know anything about her."

"My wife's not historically minded. I'm afraid I must bore her terribly, poring over the births and deaths in the church records."

"They go back that far?"

"Oh, yes. Most interesting. The minister can be very accommodating if anyone's anxious to see them. The manse is in the copse behind the church. I don't suppose you saw it. It's hidden all summer when the trees are in full leaf."

"No, I didn't."

"Well, don't be afraid to make yourself known. I realize what a troubled time you must be having. He's very understanding, old Mr. Kennedy."

It was almost too easy to talk to Sir Richard. Frances had an uneasy feeling that both Lady Hallowes's and Aunt Bessie's eyes were upon them from behind the screening lace curtains.

Neither might be very pleased that she and the master of the house were getting on so well.

"I think I should be getting ready for luncheon," she said.

"Leave your stuff here. No one's likely to touch anything. Empty that water over the flower bed. You'll want fresh when you come back. It's beginning to look a little murky."

"I will, it that's all right."

"Pity there aren't a few young people here to entertain you. But Martin's a lone wolf, and anyway, he's off on some ploy for the next week or so." Sir Richard sounded regretful, but Frances couldn't decide whether it was on account of his son's being a lone wolf or because Martin was going to be away. The description sounded like Martin, whose appearance usually suggested elements of danger.

Sir Richard strode away, a lonely figure, and Frances found herself pitying him. Neither Lady Hallowes nor her son were comfortable people. He'd lost Simon. But there really wasn't time to brood over what didn't concern her, however strongly Simon was taking over her thoughts. There was Aunt Bessie waiting for her, ready to show disapproval if she wasn't fresh and tidy and on time for her meal. When she had her own home, Frances thought, food would wait upon events. There'd be no such strict timetable. Sighing, she went indoors.

CHAPTER SIX

Frances painted several more pictures while the weather remained fine, mostly of the Hallowes roses. She didn't see Sir Richard again, but the house felt more comfortable without Martin in it. Deliberately, she tired herself out each day so that the oddness of the nursery had no real chance to disturb her at bedtime. Mary always came with the brass can of hot water and brushed her hair and talked for a little. Her father was a gamekeeper, and her mother worked in the wash house, which Frances hadn't yet seen. Mary had two older brothers, one a boot boy and the other a stable lad.

Frances had almost forgotten the strange business of the finding and subsequent theft of the ring.

The rains came on the sixth day after Martin's departure, at first small and grudging, surrounding the castle in a cloud of mist, then increasing to a deluge that hammered on the roof and hissed into the dry ground.

She wrote another, longer letter to Papa, enclosing yet another piece of St. John's Wort and a lock of her hair. Then, spreading her painting things on the table in her room, she began to stroke in a picture of the branches that overhung the window. Moonbranches, she thought. Moonbranches. The thought was like a whisper, a voice in her mind. Someone else had spoken those words. Someone in this room, long, long ago.

She had the clearest picture of Simon standing in front of the window where the branches of the great tree met. His face was happy, and he seemed to be speaking to someone just out of sight. Frances felt that she loved that smiling face, that there was goodness in it and as much intelligence as Martin showed, though of a vastly different nature. Just for a moment Simon was looking at her with pleased recognition, but then the picture shivered and he was gone. But she knew then that the past lived on, and the conviction both disturbed and comforted her. Long-ago happenings couldn't be blotted out, either good or bad. Hallowes seemed haunted by the latter.

Her recollections of the ring became very strong again, and she wondered how she could have treated its loss so lightly. If Martin had a greater right to it, why hadn't he told her? But, of course, she'd never told him or anyone else that it was found. Yet he'd known, as he seemed to know almost everything.

She stared at the picture of the branches, and her spine crept. The rain glided almost solidly over the windowpane, so that the gorge became a shadowy mass of a hundred differing greens and grays, an unknown landscape.

She put the brush into the water jar. Mary was coming upstairs. Frances had learned to recognize her step, which was solid and reassuring—not like Jenny's, which was light and rather sly, as though she hoped to catch Frances out in some misdemeanor.

"Mrs. Crabbe says, do you want your fire lit?" Mary said, poking her head around the door. Her down-to-earth common sense always made Frances a little ashamed of her imaginings.

"In summer?" Frances was amazed.

"It does get very cold inside on damp days."

"I must be hardy. I don't seem to feel it."

"Just come down if you change your mind. Goodness, you do paint well, Miss Frances."

"I seemed to improve once I arrived here."

"A pity you won't be able to go into the garden—maybe for days—because of the dratted rain. It doesn't look as if *that* will improve!"

"Oh, that reminds me, Lady Hallowes said I might explore the attics if the weather was bad. She said you'd show me the door."

"Do you really want to go into them dusty places? It's scary in there. I had to go once, not long ago, looking for a bedpan when Sir Richard's old aunt was taken ill at Hallowes. Glad to get out, I was."

"I've had enough of painting for today, and I don't want to trouble my aunt. Yes, I do want you to show me. You needn't go in yourself."

Mary picked up the strike-light and began to light the lamp. "You'll need this. There's only a couple of small skylights, and they're smeared over with smoke from the chimneys. Best thing to do is to set it down on that old chest of drawers. Then it's sort of in the middle of the long attic."

"Is it a good floor?"

"Oh, yes. Dusty and splintery, but you won't put your foot through."

"Lady Hallowes mentioned some old clothes."

"I never noticed those, miss. I just didn't like it up there, and all I wanted was to get out again as fast as I could."

"Do you like Spanish?"

"Yes, miss. Don't get too much of it."

"There you are." Frances gave Mary a piece of the hard licorice stick.

"Shouldn't really, miss, you spoil me. I haven't opened the sweets tin yet. It seems a shame to, but when I do, you must have the first."

"We'll see! I may not be here then."

Mary stopped smiling. "It'll seem odd, not having you in the nursery."

"I'll go back to school at the end of the summer."

"Oh, but you'll come back again, won't you? Of course, you'll be wanting to have your father back. Only natural."

"Yes. That's what I want." Some of the pleasure of anticipation went out of the afternoon.

"Don't look so sad, miss. I mentioned him in my prayers. I'll do it every night." Mary took up the lamp. "Come on, better you than me."

Frances followed her out of the room and along the narrow passage flanking the silent schoolroom and deserted bedrooms. The tap still dripped, but she almost welcomed the now-familiar sound. *Drop, drop, drop, splash. Drop, drop, drop, splash.* Waltzing, Frances thought dreamily, waltzing in a white gown with broderie anglaise, her long hair brushing her arm. . . .

"This is it," Mary said, coming to a halt outside a low green-painted door, up a short flight of steps.

Frances wasn't quite sure how she'd come to be there, she'd been so immersed in the fancy that she was dancing very slowly under a misted chandelier, and that arms had encircled her waist. That Simon had watched her lovingly and that she thought of him in the same way.

"Thank you, Mary." She took hold of the lamp and Mary pushed open the door to reveal a brownish gray dimness and a plethora of roof beams. Gingerly, Frances stepped inside.

"You're sure you don't want me to go in with you?" Mary asked with marked distaste.

"Oh, no. I'm sure my aunt expects you back in the kitchen, doesn't she? You'd better do that." Frances's voice sounded hollow, echoing between the beams.

"Very well, miss."

Frances heard Mary retreat, her footsteps becoming very distant, merging in with the silence of the attic. Or was it so silent? She thought she heard the faintest swish, like the drag of a skirt over a floor overhead. But there was no floor above, only the gray slates of the roof. A bird, perhaps? But a bird was light, and its feet would be soundless through the thickness of heavy slate.

Now that her eyes had become accustomed to the darkness, she could see the shapes of old chairs and picture frames, a wooden cradle on rockers. The chest of drawers mentioned by Mary loomed in the middle distance, and she began to walk toward it, her gaze held by a succession of objects barely touched by the pale glow of the small lamp. She kicked some small article that rolled away into the shadows and was lost.

Beside the chest of drawers, a trunk, its lid open and

resting against the wall, disgorged a variety of trailing garments. Frances set down the lamp as Mary had suggested. Beyond the chest a gray-painted rocking horse seemed to be staring at her with stolid surprise. She went to it and pushed tentatively. It moved easily with the barest creaking. *Creak, swish, creak, swish, creak—* The red stirrups seemed oddly distended, as though unseen feet urged the dappled creature to greater effort.

Her heart thudded. Frances told herself not to be stupid and turned her back to the horse. *Creak, swish, creak—* When the horse stopped, the silence was almost worse than the sound. Then she forgot the horse.

A white gown hung over the edge of the trunk, its bodice and hem embroidered in white thread around small holes. She knelt to touch the starched, crumpled folds, and it felt curiously familiar. Frances knew that if she turned the dress over, the string that ran through the inside of the waist would be frayed at one end. A minute passed by, two minutes, then she nerved herself to look. It was. A wild fear possessed her. She threw the dress down, wanting to rush back to the small green door, but her legs refused to carry her. Yet in spite of her fear, she felt impelled to pick up the dress a second time. Slowly, she controlled the terror that had filled her. It wasn't unreasonable to imagine that an old garment would be partly worn, and tie-strings were always fraying, like bootlaces. There was no black magic.

She held out the dress. Surely she recognized the design? There was no denying that it both looked and felt familiar. But a lady on the train had lent her a women's journal, and there had been a section that dealt with old fashions. Perhaps one of them had looked just like this. Papa had told her that there was nothing as odd and selective as the human brain, and there was no knowing when a fact, once there, would jump out like a jack-in-the-box when least expected.

And there had been that vivid dream. Though she had only seen the skirt and hem of the dress in the dream, it had looked like this one.

Her mind fastened on something Mary had said about the old clothes. Mary said she hadn't noticed them when she was in the attic, but she *had* put the lamp on top of this old chest of drawers. How could she have missed the open trunk and the half-spilled garments? They lay directly under the strongest light, less than a foot away.

Someone must have opened the trunk since then. Mary had told her that it was only a short time ago that Sir Richard's aunt had taken to her bed while visiting. So, the clothes had to have been recently removed.

Frances suspected that the other maids would be as unwilling as Mary to venture into the attics, and that even if they'd done so in the nature of a dare, they'd never have left the garments this way. They'd have refolded them and closed the lid.

Frances put down the white dress and picked up a plum-colored velvet jacket trimmed with dingy lace and bits of tarnished gold braid. It smelled vaguely of damp and traces of sweat. She supposed that it must have been much more difficult to clean such garments in the days when this coat was worn. She lifted a pair of fawn breeches, white, crumpled stockings, once-white bodices with drawstring necks and waists and yellowing folds, a fan of lace, ivory with age and smelling of musk.

Overcome by a complusion to try on the white dress, she slipped off her skirt and removed her blouse. It wasn't as if she didn't have permission to be here, and it wasn't at all unusual for a young girl to want to try on something from the past. Most of these garments had probably been worn at fancy-dress parties. And there remained the memory of the dream in which she'd danced with Simon and been drawn irresistibly toward him, almost as though some strong bond had existed between them. She'd never felt like that about anyone else. She couldn't bear to face up to the realization that he was dead. But through her dreams, he continued to ask her for help. Help to do what? At least in sleep he still belonged to her.

She pulled up the bodice of the dress and wished that she could fasten it properly, but the frayed drawstring was too short. Over in the corner an old mirror leaned against the wall, dingy and with some of the silvering worn off. Holding the back of the dress against her, she looked at her distorted reflection. In the shadows of the attic she was little more than a silhouette, a stranger, her mind filled with strange fancies and even odder memories. She could recall Hallowes when it was newer and the trees were young.

Her fingers held the sensations of picking damsons and peaches and herbs from a special plot. She could almost smell rosemary and thyme, the heady scent of apples laid away for winter.

Don't forget Simon. The thought obliterated everything else. You musn't forget Simon. As if she could, having felt his warmth, having recognized his need. Simon . . .

Frances went on staring at the mirror, all of her being concentrated on Simon Hallowes, half-imagining that his dim reflection lingered behind her own. But was it her own? She touched the cold glass and was brought back sharply to the present. Moving away, she picked up the fan, examining the fine carving on the ivory handles, trying to still the heavy beating of her heart.

She extended the fan and fluttered it to and fro like an enormous butterfly. The wafted air sent up little eddies of dust to prick at her nose. Frances sneezed several times.

Behind her somebody laughed very softly.

She whirled around, staring, the fan dangling from her hand. A tall, slim figure was outlined against the open door to the top of the staircase. The face was lost in darkness, but she knew that it was Martin.

"You said you'd be gone a week."

"Oh, dear. That sounds rather like an accusation."

"I'm sorry. It wasn't meant that way."

"But it was, wasn't it." Martin began to walk toward her, his silhouette getting larger and larger until Frances felt oppressed by his nearness. His features came into focus, faintly yellowed like the old cotton and cambric, his mouth twisted into a grin.

He leaned against the wall, his fingers reaching out to tug at the bars of the rusted birdcage that loomed out of the dimness. The thin bars twanged eerily, reminding her of the tap music. Particles of rust fell to the bottom of the cage like flakes of dried blood.

"Your mother said I might come up to the attics," Frances said, fighting the sensation of faintness brought on by his proximity, forestalling any attempt by Martin to dispute her right to be there.

"It suits Mama to make a show of generosity."

"You never have a good word to say for your mother!

You should be glad you have one. I haven't." Anger drove out the fear.

"We're at the age when feet of clay begin to show. You'd have found out things about yours to criticize, I daresay."

"I hope I should have been more charitable."

"You can't know. Not for sure." Martin smiled.

It annoyed her that there was no ready answer.

"Mama wore that once, at a fancy-dress ball. I could see her from the stairs. We both could." Martin stared at the white gown with the broderie anglaise, as though picturing his mother wearing it.

"Both?" Frances retreated a step.

"Simon and I. It was the Christmas before—"

"Before he drowned," Frances finished for him.

There was a sudden wash of heavy rain over the sky-lights. "Right on cue," Martin said mockingly, raising his eyes to the streaming glass. The rain hissed like a curling wave, and Frances found herself foolishly ducking out of the way, so strong was the sensation of being in danger.

"Mama was waltzing," Martin murmured, his attention returning to the white dress. "She had her hair loose, and she seemed to be waltzing all evening. It's very old. More than a hundred years. Papa says it was Francesca's." His soft voice echoed against the rafters.

"Francesca's?"

"Oh, you know who she was, don't you! Papa told you about her. She painted roses and—died untimely."

Died untimely. It was terrible to think of a young girl dying before her life had properly begun, but Martin's voice reflected nothing of pity. No doubt he'd have referred to his

brother in much the same tone if there'd been the necessity
to speak of Simon.

The force of her outrage broke against the stifling confines
of the attic. Frances pushed against the horse, sending it creaking and plunging. She ran past Martin, and the folds of the
white gown felt strange against her skin, like living cobwebs.

She stopped at the door and looked back. Martin was
standing out of range of the lamp, dark and faceless, but still
she knew that he was smiling.

"You took the ring from my drawer," she shouted.

"And what are you going to do about it?"

She fancied she detected a faint note of unease in his
voice, and she disliked herself for her moment of triumph.

"I haven't quite decided," she told him, quiet now. "But
I'll think of something."

"I'll deny everything."

"Naturally. But remember that I can describe it. There
can't be many such rings."

"I'll remind my parents that Mary comes up to your room
every evening. She has plenty of opportunities to pry. You
aren't always there. Maids rather like to see what guests keep
in their chests of drawers. A moment of temptation—?"

"Mary wouldn't!"

"It would be her word against mine. I shouldn't say anything if I were you. Better to let sleeping dogs lie, eh?"

She fought back the impulse to return and strike him,
but that would accomplish nothing. Slowly she went down
to the nursery floor. The rain had slackened, and from the
schoolroom she could see the edge of a rainbow, but the sight
did nothing to cheer her. Martin had come back, and peace
had fled.

It was several minutes before she remembered that she was still wearing the dress, Francesca's gown, and she hurried back to change into her own clothes.

Martin had gone, but he had left his own special aura about the shadowy attics, a compound of wickedness and a terrible pleasure in its effect on others.

She could hardly wait to get away.

CHAPTER SEVEN

Lady Hallowes sent for Frances again the next morning, and she went to answer the summons with mixed feelings. Not that she really thought Martin had mentioned their encounter. He was obviously anxious that the business of the ring remain a secret between them.

"Mrs. Kennedy, the minister's wife, has unearthed a good many copies of *The Girl's Own Paper*," Lady Hallowes told Frances, her lovely face unlined by any of the problems Frances had envisaged. "She sent a pile for you, which one of the maids is putting in your room. Perhaps you'd be a good girl and call to thank her. She kept them from her own childhood, and Scottish weather being what it is, you might bless them before long."

"That was kind. I most certainly will."

"You must allow me to see your paintings. My husband says you have genuine talent." Lady Hallowes lifted a lace-draped hand to smooth her dark red hair. "And I may say that Richard seldom praises without good reason."

"Oh dear. I don't know what to say!"

"Have I embarrassed you? But he was so enthusiastic, I thought you should know."

"Perhaps I could give you and your husband the picture you like most out of the ones I manage to finish before I leave?"

"I should certainly like to look at them, at least. Oh, and if you are free on Friday next, could I ask you to go back to Mr. McGregor's?"

"Mr. McGregor?"

"The pharmacist. For my bottle."

"Oh, yes. I'd planned to have another trip to the village, so it might as well be Friday."

"Very well. I can leave that in your hands, then, can I? I know Roberts wants to be off. A family wedding."

"I won't forget." Frances wondered if Roberts was the man who'd driven her from the station.

Lady Hallowes gave Frances one of her mysterious Morgan Le Fay smiles, and Frances imagined her with her hair hanging loose, dancing in the broderie anglaise gown under a Waterford chandelier. Before Simon died.

She hated to think of Simon Hallowes being dead. Wasn't it stupid to imagine herself even a little in love with a ghost? Frances thought of Simon all the way up the stairs to her room, but forgot him once she was there and saw the huge pile of magazines on the chest in the corner.

Fascinated, she discovered that the vicar's wife had kept the first copy, dated January 3, 1880. Thirty-five years ago! There was a picture of a young Queen Victoria on the front, looking very small and childish apart from her heavy-lidded eyes.

Flipping through page after page, Frances was struck by an illustration for a Christmas play that showed Father Christmas overshadowed by a ghostly figure who was meant to represent Fog; he was swathed in a dark voile, out of which two small eyes stared inimically. Even an attractive article entitled "How to Make the Most of Your Holiday" and depicting a pleasant lady sitting on huge rocks, a young girl at her side painting, couldn't entirely diminish the impact of Fog.

By the time she'd reached the warnings about the fearful dangers awaiting girls who contemplated the stage as a career, as contrasted with the vastly different and laudable ambition of becoming a nurse, Frances was thoroughly immersed in the magazine. One title page in particular pleased her. Illustrated by Kate Greenaway, it depicted the seated figures of three young women set in a border of flower posies: pink roses and a white lily, some spring flowers, autumnal blooms, and even a sprig of well-berried holly.

For the first time, Frances thought of using her own penchant for art as a possible means of making a living. If Sir Richard wasn't just being kind, her talent might be worth fostering. He'd be unlikely to praise her work to his wife unless he felt reasonably strongly about the watercolors he'd seen.

But self-doubt made Frances turn instead to advice on the illicit but accepted pleasures of lip salves and rose glycerine as opposed to those enemies of womanly modesty, powder and paint. Cold baths were suitable and beneficial, provided one didn't use colored or strongly scented soaps. Better by far to go out on a May morning and press one's face to the dewy grass. But what of the other three hundred and sixty-four mornings? she wondered, and found herself giggling. By the time she'd digested the delicious gruesomeness of washing the hair in not one but two freshly laid egg yolks, and expanding the chest with a device obtainable from a surgeon's mechanic, whatever that was, or from an india rubber warehouse, Frances was laughing out loud, something she hadn't done since she was last at school.

She passed enjoyably to the perils of tight lacing and a graphic picture of a fallen man straddled by an oversized tiger, being shot at by a lady most unsuitably dressed for the dense jungle that surrounded her. Did *anyone* wear a bustle and a large-brimmed hat festooned with ribbons and flowers under such circumstances? Yet *could* one say, "I must dress sensibly today in case Guy should be attacked by a predator"? The prone gentleman was certain to be called something like Guy, or Arnold, or Vivian.

Perhaps she should become a writer? If an inflated imagination was anything to go by, she might make a reasonably good job of such an occupation.

Frances stopped turning the pages abruptly. She stared at the picture of a dark station, a murky train almost obscured by red-coated soldiers bidding farewell to a sad huddle of women and children, while an old man held out one hand in a futile gesture of reclamation. Kit bags—weapons—drifting steam. Pain—

She closed the magazine quickly, all inclination to laugh swept away in a brutal recollection of parting with her father. She stared at the clock on the mantel. Over an hour had passed since she'd sat down with these old, nostalgic copies. She felt ashamed that she'd been enjoying herself while Papa was engaged in keeping himself alive. It was useless to tell herself that he'd prefer her to entertain herself harmlessly.

Staring out of the window, she saw that the rain had

almost stopped. There would be time for a walk before lunch. Resolutely, she put on her strongest waterproof boots and let herself out of the house. Trees dripped and the ground squelched a little. Avoiding the south wood, she made her way to the beach, which looked desolate under the gray sky. Nothing moved but the waves and a few distant birds, but she felt more alive down here than up in her room. The sand was firm under her feet, and the far-off shape of the church beckoned.

Soon she was quite close enough to see the gravestones, Simon's so fresh and white, Francesca's dark and slightly tilted, the lettering entirely illegible this gloomy morning; only the little circles of orange lichen were bright and glowing against so much that was somber.

Letting herself out by the small black gate, she followed a vaguely indicated path to the right, and soon found herself able to see the shadow of a house beyond the proliferation of wet leaves that gave it perfect concealment from prying eyes.

It was a gloomy building, the stone dark and forbidding, half-concealed by ivy that grew high as though in an attempt to throttle both drainpipes and windows. Large, as most Victorian manses were, and oversized for the small, much older church, it was obviously a replacement for some previous tumbledown dwelling. The Kennedys must find it a problem to heat in winter, she thought, and if they aren't a large family, they must rattle about in it like peas in a pod.

A middle-aged lady in dark, serviceable clothes was rooting about with a trowel in a soggy flower bed under the front window. She looked up as Frances approached, and her weatherbeaten face was kind. Her gray eyes scrutinized Frances with what seemed to be approval as she got up, supporting herself with one hand on the sill, the other rubbing the small of her back.

"I came to see Mrs. Kennedy," Frances told her.

"I'm Mrs. Kennedy. You must be Mrs. Crabbe's niece."

Frances nodded. "It was about the books—"

"That was nothing. They were taking up far too much room. Look, I'm about to have a cup of tea. Please have one with me? That's enough gardening for one morning."

"Are you sure I'm not interrupting anything?"

"You aren't, so that's settled." Mrs. Kennedy brushed at a wisp of gray hair with her forearm to avoid soiling her brow with earth-stained hands.

"I suppose I ought to wear gloves, but that takes away some of the elemental pleasure." The minister's wife led the way around the side of the house and through a gloomy room equipped with sinks and a long deal table cluttered with flowerpots and chipped enamel jugs, mud-stained trowels and dead leaves.

Frances was asked to sit in a small morning room while Mrs. Kennedy went to wash her hands and make tea. The wallpaper was dark, and the room was filled with whatnots covered with sepia-tinted photographs: uneasy, straight-backed ladies with small waists and impressive bosoms restrained by chastely buttoned bodices, their necks and busts ornamented with hair brooches and the dark glitter of jet; and mutton-chopped, bewhiskered and bearded gentlemen with glazed eyes and alberts stretched across their waistcoats, all staring unnervingly at some point just out of sight of the camera.

"Funny old lot, they are," Mrs. Kennedy said cheerfully, making Frances jump. She'd been so absorbed that she hadn't

75

heard the minister's wife return. Mrs. Kennedy put a tray down on a rather battered pie-crust table.

"Your relations?" Frances inquired.

"Good gracious, no! We didn't have the time or inclination to force ourselves into such uncomfortable garments. Besides, you can't garden in a corset that cuts you in two. I believe in comfort and wearing the clothes for the job in hand. Now you look just right, my dear. Sensible, yet quite charming. I like simplicity."

"Whose are they, then?" Frances indicated the photographs.

"Old Mr. Forbes's, our predecessor. He hadn't a soul in the world when he died, and I hadn't the heart to sweep out the past so unkindly. Things that have meant a good deal to a person shouldn't be destroyed just because they clutter up the place. I daresay when we go, they'll be thrown out, but I couldn't do it. Milk and sugar?"

"Neither, please, just a little extra hot water."

"But you will have some seedcake?"

"Yes, please." The seedcake looked a little dry but Frances couldn't refuse. It would have put her on the same plane as someone who could jettison pictures of someone else's dead relatives.

Mrs. Kennedy handed her the cake and looked fondly at the galaxy of dim brown faces. "I've got so attached to them, really. It's almost as though we were connected. I even have names for them all. Like Mr. Forbes, Jamie and I won't leave anyone behind. The last of both lines, we are. There was a son, once. . . . " Her voice faded.

Frances didn't like to ask what had become of the Kennedys' son, so she took a bite of seedcake. It stuck in her throat and brought on a fit of coughing that made her face red and her eyes water. Mrs. Kennedy jumped up and slapped her firmly on the back, and by the time Frances had managed to get down some tea to stifle the discomfort, the subject of the Kennedys' boy was safely shelved.

Mrs. Kennedy chattered on and soon knew all there was to be known about Frances. "I'm glad you like the GOPs." She pronounced it "gops." "You don't want to be sitting about brooding."

"GOPs?"

"That's what they nicknamed the girl's paper. The whole name always was a bit of a mouthful, I suppose."

"Well, there's one thing, I'll never have another dull moment. There's a lot of reading there."

"Has it been dull?"

"Not really," Frances said quickly. It would never do if Lady Hallowes received the notion that she was dissatisfied.

"Lady Hallowes is quite impressed by you, and Sir Richard by your painting. It must be very fulfilling to have such a gift."

Frances wondered how to explain that this talent had only really surfaced when she came to Hallowes. At home her painting had not been at all exceptional. "He did say that he was reminded of the work of someone called Francesca—"

There was the sound of a scuffle in the passage, and a masculine voice said, "Behave yourself, Brutus. Are you in there, Amelia?"

"We're having tea. I brought a cup for you," Mrs. Kennedy called. "But I think it's time this cake was relegated to the bird table. Poor little Miss Frances has all but choked to death on it."

77

"Dear, dear." A head poked round the door. "We can't have that. I hope you won't be put off by that, child."

Blue eyes twinkled from a face considerably older than his wife's, but like hers, there was kindness in the expression. Frances decided that she liked the Kennedys.

"I'll just put Brutus in the kitchen. He's liberally bespattered with mud."

Mr. Kennedy departed, and his wife gathered up what remained of the offending cake and put it on a side table. "We don't think too much about food," she confessed. "I'm far too much involved with my flowers and the birds in the garden and on the shore. There are some magnificent shrubs and trees around Hallowes."

"I noticed some unusual ones beside the pool. That dark pool under the bridge."

A shadow crossed Mrs. Kennedy's face. "Ah, yes. The pool."

"And from the nursery windows. At least two of the trees reach the edge of the roof. The branches tap on the glass when there's any vestige of wind."

"Poor little Simon," Mrs. Kennedy murmured, almost as though Frances weren't there. "He was a lovely boy. I'd lost my own, but for a while Simon gave back a little of what was gone forever." She said nothing at all about Martin. There seemed to be no one with a good word for Simon's brother. Then she went on, "It was all the fault of that wretched Luck. As though such objects really can have any influence on our lives. Downright ungodly, I'd call it."

"Luck?"

"An odd ring the Halloweses possessed. It was an ugly thing. Some ancestor had brought the stone back from Australia. A whopping big opal with the most garish colors, but some folks said they could see things in it. I never could, but I'm not blessed with overmuch imagination. They had it set into a ring, and it became a sort of talisman."

Frances sat frozen. She'd seen the Luck, touched it, owned it for a brief space, had sensed its strange power.

"It killed Simon. Oh, not through any sort of black magic or supernatural mumbo jumbo. He accidentally dropped it in the pool and foolishly tried to get it back."

"Is that what Martin said? He was there, wasn't he."

"He saw it all. Both boys set great store by the ring, but it was Simon's inheritance, his being the older of the two. I'll say this for Martin: He did try his best to fetch help. I've never seen anyone so distraught."

Martin was a good actor, Frances thought, then despised herself for her lack of charity. But how could he have seen the ring fall into the pool when it was found in the wood?

"Did they get the Luck back again?"

"There was no way. The pool's deceptively deep and very dark, extremely dangerous. It must be buried in silt."

Frances found that her heart was beating very fast and hurting her rib cage. Had something else fallen into the pool, something that Simon had mistaken for the ring, or—? The last question was so terrible that she felt a little faint.

Mr. Kennedy's feet scuffed the flagstones in the passageway, and Frances was forced to thrust the monstrous thought away from her and produce a pale smile.

The minister sat down with a contented sigh, accepting a cup of tea from his wife with evident pleasure.

"I have to drive him out," Mrs. Kennedy complained, "or he'd never have any fresh air and exercise."

"I do my duty. House calls—"

"House calls! That's not fresh air. Stuffy rooms, sick-rooms! Overcrowded rooms."

"I do have to make my way there."

"It's still not the same as a good, vigorous stride along the beach, throwing sticks for Brutus," Mrs. Kennedy said firmly. "You look all the better for it, Jamie, and you'll sleep well tonight."

"And what brings you to the manse?" the minister asked, transferring his blue gaze to Frances.

"To thank Mrs. Kennedy for the GOPs."

He frowned.

The Girl's Own Papers, daftie!" Mrs. Kennedy said, and laughed. "My husband lives up on another plane. Are you in such a hurry to reach heaven?"

"You mustn't joke about such things, Amelia."

"I'm sure God won't mind our having a little fun on earth. What do you think, Frances?"

"And you really shouldn't embroil the girl in our differences." Mr. Kennedy sounded good-natured but just as firm as his wife had been over the fresh air and beachwalking.

Mrs. Kennedy produced a tin containing a few rather elderly looking abernethy biscuits. "Jamie?"

Mr. Kennedy took one absently, but Frances, remembering the coughing fit, refused politely.

"And how do you find life at Hallowes?" the minister inquired.

Frances looked at the brown photographs for inspiration. One of the faces that stared back at her reminded her of somebody, but before recognition could properly crystallize, she realized that Mr. Kennedy required an answer.

"Everyone's been very kind."

"As if she could possibly say anything else," Mrs. Kennedy murmured.

"Sir Richard suggested I might speak to you about Francesca. He says you have the old church records."

"Yes, I have. They were kept locked up in the vestry until we had an attempted burglary, then I moved them into my study. How did you come to hear of Francesca Hallowes?"

"Sir Richard said my flower paintings were like hers, and I also had noticed her tombstone. Then I discovered that I wanted to know more about the family. Could I see the old parish books? I'd be very careful."

"I don't see why not, Jamie. No one ever asks to see them nowadays, apart from Sir Richard, and if he trusts Frances, I don't see why you shouldn't."

"Well, I do have to write my sermon. I could get on with that at the bureau, and young Miss Frances could have the records on the large desktop. How would that suit you, young lady?"

"And don't strain your eyes," Mrs. Kennedy ordered, not unkindly. "Like the scrawlings of a rheumaticky spider, some of those entries. They make my head ache."

"Be off and see to your garden, woman."

"See how he addresses me?" But Mrs. Kennedy didn't look too put out about being summarily dismissed. "I'll let you know when it gets near lunchtime."

The study was on the other side of the corridor from the dark morning room, and, being paneled and lined with books, even darker. Surrounding trees shut out a good deal of daylight. Mr. Kennedy groped behind a white bust of Sir Walter Scott to bring out a strike-light. The desk became bathed in the soft radiance of a pink-shaded oil lamp.

"There," Mr. Kennedy told Frances. "That should be better." Taking out a small key, he unlocked a tall, brown cupboard and extracted a large black book, which he laid carefully on the desk. "You may, as Amelia says, find certain portions difficult to read, but there's a magnifying glass on the desk. Most of these entries are for farmers and village folk. It's a scattered parish. I'll just give you one at a time."

"Thank you." Frances, trying to conceal her feelings of excitement, sat down and ran her fingers over the dingy cover before opening the book. Part of her mind was aware of Mr. Kennedy and the way his clothes rustled and his boots squeaked as he crossed the floor; the rest was concentrating fiercely on having achieved part of her growing necessity to solve the mysteries of Francesca and Simon.

Mrs. Kennedy had been right about the poor quality of the earlier penmanship. Frances had to hold the magnifying glass above the page. The scrawled entries tore at her heart.

1774, 23rd April, Jane, daughter of George Macdonald

1775, Oct 2nd, Grace, daughter of George Macdonald

1777, June 25th, Mary, daughter of George Macdonald

1778, April 4th, Robert, son of George Macdonald

How had he borne it? And what of his wife, their mother? Four children lost in as many years. Worse still was a record dated January 8, 1780. A stranger, name not known. Was it

82

a man or a woman who had arrived at the village in the cold of winter, only to meet with death?

Sometimes the cause of death appeared—smallpox, bowel complaint, consumption—or the sum of the people's years was given and one knew that old age had carried them off. In September 1796 a male child was found dead, name unknown. Frances hadn't realized that such laconic reports could carry such a weight of pathos. At least the stranger had lived, not like the tiny September baby.

Suddenly she stopped reading the ill-written, crabbed lines. Francesca Hallowes, 18 years, on July 29, 1799, died of a girl child. Francesca. Girl child. Died untimely. Over and over again the stark words rang in her mind.

Mr. Kennedy was writing. His pen flew over the paper like an angry bird, and she realized that there was something else under the kindness, something strong that insisted upon coming to the surface and that would be spoken in the little church next Sunday. He stopped as though aware of the fact that she was listening. "Is everything all right?"

"Yes," she replied, though everything seemed all wrong when an eighteen-year-old girl could die while giving birth to a baby. "Could I —would it be too much trouble to see the register of births?"

"No trouble at all." Mr. Kennedy rose and came to the desk. "Are you finished with this one?"

"Oh, yes. Thank you."

He gave her another black-covered tome and returned to his sermon, though when he resumed his writing, she noticed that some of the almost angry urgency had gone out of it.

Frances turned the pages carefully until she came to the entries for the 1790s. It seemed very important that she discover whether or not the child had survived. The pages were filled with Macdonalds and Frasers, Mackintoshes and Robertsons. Then, there it was, seeming to have been written in darker ink than the rest. Frances Louise, daughter of Francesca Hallowes, July 29, 1799. No mention of her dying, only of having been born on the same day that her mother departed this life. What had happened to her? Probably nothing more prosaic than being brought up by her father, or the Hallowes grandparents.

Frances closed the book just as Mrs. Kennedy looked in to tell her that it was nearly lunchtime but that she could always come back whenever she wished.

"Successful, were you?"

"Oh, quite," Frances told the minister's wife a little emptily, then added a thank-you in case they imagined her ungrateful.

"I thought I must remind you. Mrs. Crabbe is a stickler for punctuality."

"Yes, she is. I simply must fly." Frances grabbed her hat and found Mr. Kennedy staring at her fixedly. All the way to the door she remembered that searching look. Mrs. Kennedy bade her a good-natured farewell and the door closed, leaving Frances standing in a veritable gale that tugged at her skirt and petticoats and tore at the ends of her hair.

But there was no time to think about the wind's sudden advent or about Francesca. A glance at her fob watch sent Frances running for the track through the north wood, her straw hat carried in her hand so it shouldn't blow away and add to her fault of dilatoriness.

CHAPTER EIGHT

Aunt Bessie had not been pleased. The fish was overdone and the pudding soggy because of the delay. Frances, her eyes already tired from the effects of reading the cramped writing in the record books, lay down on her bed after lunch, her spirits subdued because of her aunt's evident displeasure and the morning's discoveries.

She had toyed with the idea of looking at other issues of the GOPs, but decided to leave those for later, when her eyes had had a chance to recover.

The water music sounded very faintly, as though Lady Hallowes had sent someone to look at the dripping tap who had not quite succeeded in stopping the flow. The quiet notes dropped into Frances's mind as though into a pool. The dark pool, she reflected, and shivered. They all thought the ring lay at the bottom of that pool, but now Martin Hallowes had it, as he'd always intended. People imagined that he'd tried to save Simon, but Frances conjured up a vastly different picture. Simon pleading for help but Martin smiling and pushing at him with the stick. Pushing him away from the bank. Away from safety. Murdering him.

She experienced the terrible conviction that Martin had indeed killed his twin brother, to obtain possession of the Luck.

Her finger burned suddenly as though the ring still encircled it, and her palm was cold. She wanted to open her eyes but they seemed weighted with lead. Frances tried to get up but her limbs refused to obey. The tap water played a little mocking arpeggio and faded to nothingness.

Out of the darkness came a faint orange glow that deepened gradually into the deep scarlet of the desert in the ring. A purple sky brooded. For a time no one moved in the flamboyant landscape, and then Frances saw two figures in the distance. As she watched, concentrating on their slowly approaching forms, she saw that one of them was a girl in a long gown that should have been white but reflected the red glow of the sand, and the other was a boy who was in most ways the image of Martin. The girl had a look of Sir Richard—the same level gaze and high-arched cheekbones—and her nose was a fraction long, with just the hint of a bump on the bridge that took away any suggestion of severity.

Frances tried to say "Simon?" but they seemed not to hear. It was as though, once having had access to the ring, she was allowed to see them, but only regaining ownership might make her real and visible in their eyes.

They wandered aimlessly, forever peering into the empty distances as though in search of something of great importance.

"Simon!"

This time the force of her effort to attract Simon's attention had greater impact, and he stared at the place where Frances stood, peering, seeing perhaps some small shadow of reality, pulling at the girls' white sleeve and pointing, his eyes questioning.

"I'm here! Here! You asked me to come. Remember?"

"There *is* something!" Simon insisted. "Listen."

"I'm here! Frances. You called me."

But that had been in a dream, just as this was. Did one really understand such situations in dreams? Was a tiny part of her being still awake, directing her thoughts?

"It's that girl. I know it is," Simon cried out. "I'm sick to death of limbo! If it hadn't been for you, Francesca, I'd have been alone for the last nine years. Uneasy souls, they call us, and that's what we are. Now *she* knows about us. She wants to help."

Frances concentrated on the figure of the girl. So this was the eighteen-year-old who'd owned the white gown in the attic, who'd painted flowers, and died in childbed. Both of them had died untimely, haunting Hallowes because there was, as yet, nowhere for them to go, nowhere to rest. The thought upset Frances deeply. She struggled against the unhappiness this gave her, and the images of the boy and girl wavered and became part of the shifting sand and lurid sky. Then she was awake, her heart throbbing with mingled pain and frustration.

The room was dark, apart from a faint glimmer of moonlight from the direction of the window, and the thin branches scratched faintly at the panes, like fingers too weak to do anything more than merely to register their presence.

Frances got out of bed, looking out at the dark mass of the gorge, and it seemed that there were white shapes in the depth of it: two arms that waved at her before disappearing. If only she had the ring back, she thought. Having the Luck

87

would make all the difference between being on one side of an invisible wall and the other.

But how to get it back from Martin?

The house had an air of expectancy and bustle next morning. Frances, scrupulously early for breakfast but unwilling to face too much food, provoked an outburst from her aunt. "All them starving little heathens in far-off lands, and you picking at your porridge! I hope you don't intend being took ill. It wouldn't do at all just at this minute, it wouldn't, not with the family going off at a moment's notice and me with only one pair of hands."

"Going away?"

"Aye. And you bent on sickening for something."

"I'm not ill. I—didn't sleep very well. I can't help thinking about Papa—and the war."

Aunt Bessie grunted. "We all think about that, missy, but we can't let it rule our lives. It's our business to carry on as best we may, and you'd do well to remember it." Her voice was kinder now that the imagined threat of Frances's impending illness was removed. "Lady Hallowes couldn't decide whether or not to attend her niece's christening and woke up determined they should go. Until Thursday or Friday."

"And—Master Martin?"

"His papa insists that he accompany them, so they'll do some outfitting for university at the same time. As he says, it has to be done, though young Martin is more than a little displeased. Mark my words, there'll be trouble from that quarter."

Aunt Bessie went on talking, but Frances barely heard. If Martin was going away, he wouldn't dare take the ring. The ring that was supposed to be at the bottom of the black pool. There would be three or four days in which to find it, and after the housemaids had finished tidying the rooms, it seemed most unlikely that anyone would have need to enter them until just before the family returned. The Luck would almost certainly be concealed in Martin's bedroom, as he wouldn't dare leave it anywhere else.

Frances went out as soon as she could, ostensibly on her way to the beach but in reality concealed in the shrubbery to watch the carriage brought around, the boxes placed upon the rack, and the emergence of the Hallowes. Martin's mother looked most elegant in a silver gray costume and matching hat, its wide brim trimmed with silk roses, and the daintiest of gray shoes. Sir Richard presided over a Martin whose face was set with annoyance, and when Martin snapped at his mother, who had murmured something indistinguishable, he reprimanded his son curtly and told him to act like an adult instead of a six-year-old. Martin complied, his expression furious and ominous. Frances turned cold, realizing that he might well have been left behind. Martin who would stop at nothing to have his own way. Who had killed his brother.

The carriage rolled away, leaving an atmosphere of discord that was almost palpable. Frances waited in case the vehicle returned for something left behind, but the warm minutes dragged by and the distant sound of the carriage wheels died away into bee-hung silence. The front door was closed by the servants, and slowly, the aura of unrest dirfted away among the high branches. Birds returned, flirting and preening their feathers, and a blue butterfly hovered over the rhododendron blooms before settling on a glossy leaf.

Filled with a strange excitement, Frances went back inside the house by the side door, peering into the vast cavern of the kitchen and beyond to the scullery, where Mary was engaged in washing up a huge pile of dirty crockery. Aunt Bessie was elsewhere, obviously supervising the changing of the bed linen and such necessary chores, so Frances went into the dim, cheerless confines of the scullery, which was bathed in a peculiar green light fostered by the foliage that obscured much of the window.

"Can you see properly?" Frances asked doubtfully.

"Oh, yes. Tell the truth, miss, I like it. It's sort of—magic."

"I suppose it is." Frances began to wonder how best she could find out the location of Martin's room. Inspiration dawned. "You know, I never gave the other maids anything, and all of them have either brought up food or a message of some sort. I thought I might give them some Spanish or some toffee. Where would I find them at the moment?"

"They'll be halfway through the bedrooms, I shouldn't wonder. But your aunt may be there," Mary cautioned.

"I wouldn't want to disturb Aunt Bessie! Is there anywhere I could watch discreetly? I could bide my chance."

"Go up to the first floor and turn to the right. That's where the master bedroom and Master Martin's are. There's a little cubbyhole just at the beginning of the corridor, round the corner from the staircase, that's only used to store candles and polish and such-like for future use. I doubt if anyone'll go in there for weeks. It's only visited when stores run out down here, and no one's said anything recently to Mrs. Crabbe about shortages or I'd have heard."

Mary's plain, pleasant face lit up impishly at the thought of France's daring. "You'll be just like a lady detective, won't you. Hope your aunt don't find out! You wouldn't like just to leave the licorice and sweets here with me?"

"I left them upstairs." Frances experienced a flicker of shame for her deception, not that she didn't intend to give the remainder of her hoard of sweetmeats to Jenny and the others. That part of it was true. Of course, the shabby part of her behavior was forced on her by Martin's theft of the ring. But even the fact of his blackmail threats to Mary and her good name couldn't blot out the growing feelings of distaste Frances had for her own scheming. Yet, if Simon and Francesca truly depended on her to help them escape from their present unhappy situation, she needed the Luck. And she'd decided to get it! A load seemed to roll away from her heart as Frances realized that her mind was indeed quite made up. She must be as strong as Martin.

She left Mary staring after her with a kind of hero worship and began cautiously to go upstairs by the forbidden central staircase that shut off the family suite from the rest of the house. She found the little storeroom right away. The sound of voices came from the open doorways, Aunt Bessie's louder than the others. "Use a bit of elbow grease on that, Dora! There's no time for those namby-pamby ways this morning. I want these rooms finished by lunchtime. Good gracious, is that all the beeswax you've got? You should have told me before now. You're going to need more than that. Your brain doesn't carry you to the scullery and back. Get another tin from the store."

Frances's heart almost stopped with fright. There was nowhere to hide, and she didn't dare step outside. Blood rushed guiltily to her face.

"Wait, Dora. There's still a tin in the kitchen. That

drawer by the window. I know there is, because I saw it this morning when I put the cellar key away for Sir Richard. Fetch that one, because it has already been started and we don't want to open another needlessly. Hurry up, you daft creature."

Frances flinched backward as Dora ran along the corridor, even though she knew the girl couldn't see her. Was this how burglars felt when faced with discovery? Her heartbeats had quieted themselves before Dora returned, muttering crossly under her breath.

"And get down to the feet this time," Aunt Bessie commanded. "Lady Hallowes isn't blind, you know. If she dropped anything onto the carpet, whatever d'you think she'd say coming face-to-face with such carelessness?"

The exhortation and criticism continued for another ten minutes, then the corridor shook a little as the laundry cart rumbled by on its way to the small service lift.

Frances opened the storeroom door the merest crack and saw her aunt seeming to bear down upon her with an expression of ill-tempered harassment that sent her toes squirming against the leather of her boots. But Aunt Bessie sailed by, her annoyance obviously directed to some other source. She was followed a moment later by Jenny, who hesitated at the threshold of the room she'd just left, adjusted her cap at some unseen mirror, poked reflectively at her pretty hair, then closed the door, smiling secretly. She sauntered along, enjoying unspoken thoughts that Frances sensed had nothing to do with Aunt Bessie. Jenny lifted one hand to cover a small yawn and passed from sight.

The corridor was very quiet after they'd all gone. There was no sound of dripping taps on this floor, and the lack of windows, apart from the small ones at either end, muffled any of the usual outside noises of birds and insects. There was a heaviness to the atmosphere that Frances found stifling. Her heart thrusting against her rib cage, she stepped outside the cupboard and stared at the row of doors. Her feet made no sound on the thick plum-colored carpet. For the first time she noticed the ivory-colored silk wallpaper with its rich, dull sheen and self-colored pattern.

A faint smell of cooking made her remember lunch, and she looked at her fob watch. There were still ten minutes before she was expected in her aunt's sitting room, but she couldn't go without finding out which was Martin's bedroom.

She turned the first knob and stared into a chamber that was obviously his parents'. The walls were Lady Hallowes's favorite lichen green. An elegant rosewood fourposter draped in oyster and green displayed fat pillows in frilled cases bearing Sir Richard's monogram embroidered in silk in the lefthand corner. A rosewood corner stand held a Spode basin, jug, and soap dish. The bed table was also rosewood, as were the two Georgian commodes that flanked the beautiful bed and had dainty ormolu lamps and carafes of water and glasses on them. The gilt frames of the pictures glimmered. A faint, sad perfume hung in the air.

Frances closed the door quickly, feeling mean and shabby, yet charmed by the elegance of the bedchamber in spite of its suggestion of melancholy.

Slowly, she twisted the knob of the third room from which Jenny had emerged, opened the door, and stifled a scream with her free hand clamped over her mouth. Out of the shadows stared the smiling face of Martin Hallowes.

All during the midday meal, Frances felt her pulse racing

erratically. The portrait of Martin had looked so real, placed as it was in the dark recess between two windows and made even dimmer by the brilliance of light that spilled through the long panes.

The picture had been made even more striking by the suggestion of another, almost identical face that hung in the background, hardly seen at first, then, somehow emerging from a welter of grays and greens as though it intended to attract notice whether or not the painter had so intended.

Frances had been almost as shocked by the representation of Martin's lost brother as by Martin's triumphant and all-too-real features. His painted eyes held a challenge, seeming to laugh at her intention to rifle his room, promising that she'd find the task of finding the Luck beyond her power.

Aunt Bessie, after commenting on Frances's continuing lack of appetite and asking what she intended doing this afternoon without really listening to the answer, hurried off to continue those tasks that were undertaken during family absences, so as to cause the least disruption of their comfort. The drawing room was to have a complete turn-out, and everyone would be kept occupied for the next two days.

Frances gained entry to the first-floor corridor without too much difficulty, though she'd had to pick up her skirts and sprint up the last few stairs when footsteps had sounded on the black-and-white marble slabs in the hall. No one followed her.

Quietly, she slid into Martin's room and closed the door behind her. Though she tried not to look at the portrait, it was as if Martin willed her to do so. She turned away from it, her eyes searching the room for inspiration. The bed stood

94

stripped of its linen, and Frances knew that the ring wouldn't be there. The mattress would have been turned.

There were two chests, a large wardrobe, a small bedside table, and a fireside rug that concealed part of the Turkish carpet that covered all but the edges of the room. The curtains were red, to match the predominating color in the carpet, and looped back with dark blue ties. A case of butterflies and moths was fixed to one wall, and under it, standing on a small table, was a killing bottle.

Frances flinched from the sight. Each one of those beautiful insects had fluttered and died in the bottle, choked by cyanide. Another case, containing a large variety of carefully labeled birds' eggs, stood on top of one of the chests.

She hesitated, reluctant to violate the privacy of Martin's possessions. What right had she to go through with this search? What if her visions of Simon and Francesca were only dreams nurtured by an overactive imagination? Some people might say that the shock of her father's departure for the front had addled her wits or made her peculiarly vulnerable to atmosphere.

She sat on the end of the bed, her hands folded, trying to decide what she should do, where she should start her search—if she could convince herself that it was, in this case, right to pry. All sense of achievement in finding Martin's room unattended ebbed away into a kind of angry misery. There could be no doubt that the Luck was Hallowes property and Matin's inheritance, however terribly he'd arranged that.

Another five minutes passed, during which Frances fought a losing fight against her conscience. She rose, moving toward the door, then was struck motionless, her ears straining.

The sound of a girl's voice humming grew louder, then there was a snatch of singing: "Early one morning, just as the sun was rising. . ."

Frantic with the certainty that she was to be discovered where she should not be, Frances dropped to the carpet and rolled under the bed just as the door opened. From under the edge of the valance she could see a pair of small feet in black house slippers, slim ankles in black stockings.

The feet danced across the carpet and came to a halt under the portrait of Martin. "How could you use a poor maiden so?" The laughing voice finished the sad little tune, and Frances, cautiously lifting a corner of the valance, saw that the girl was Jenny, striking an impudent pose as she stared up at the pictured face. "Yes, Master Martin, it's not often your father gets the better of you. Serves you right for teasing me as you do. But I know you like me, else you wouldn't have let me come in. What I want to know is, what were you hiding last time I caught you on the hop? Something in this box."

Jenny went over to the chest where the bird collection was displayed and lifted the lid, fingering the cotton wool on which the eggs were laid, lifting the edges the better to see what might be under the fleecy white layer.

"Nothing," she said at last, her voice flat with disappointment. "Just like one of your tricks, Master Martin, to pretend you'd hid something. Though I could have sworn you were angry, with those devil's eyes glaring at me. Fair pushed me out, you did." She replaced the lid unwillingly, her pretty face frowning. "Best hurry down. Old Crabby's sure to notice I've been a long time over putting that clean glass in the master's room."

96

She sauntered to the door and, with a final dissatisfied look, went out.

It was five minutes before Frances emerged, weak with reaction, her face flushed and her hair tousled. Unsteadily, she went to the case and looked down at the bland, smooth shapes of the eggs. One of the larger ones had been shifted ever so slightly. Martin would be sure to notice.

She raised the lid and reached out to move the egg. It felt curiously light and fragile, and she felt sure that it had been broken. As she lifted it carefully, she saw that it was only half of a shell, and that something lay beneath it, something that winked flashes of red and purple from its hollow in the cotton wool.

It was the Hallowes Luck. At first she was so stunned that all she could do was to stare unbelievingly. Then she picked it up, its icy coldness burning into her warm palm, and replaced the shell with meticulous care. How cunningly Martin had dug out the undershell so that the rest would fit snugly over the ring, looking for all the world as complete as the other eggs. Sliding the ring into her pocket, she listened at the door for any further sound, looked back to make sure that the egg case was properly closed, and let herself out. All the way along the corridor she expected someone to appear, footfalls deadened by the plum-colored carpet, but no one came.

Her heart skipped a beat or two as she descended the forbidden stairs to the hall, the black-and-white floor reminding her of a giant chessboard. She found herself avoiding the black squares and making her way toward her own concealed staircase by way of the white ones.

Climbing to the nursery floor had never seemed so wea-

97

rying, like the difficult last few hundred feet below a mountaintop. It was hard to understand her tiredness when she'd spent most of the day so far skulking behind shrubs or lying under a bed.

Frances had a violent desire to giggle; yet another part of her felt stupidly weepy. Behaving deviously had been a far greater strain than she'd anticipated. She lay down on her bed before taking out the ring and slipping it on her finger.

The roses on the wallpaper shifted and spun. She closed her eyes.

She was walking on hot, red sand. Her feet dragged and her clothes stuck to her body. The dark colors of her clothing drew the heat of the sun, and there were mountains on the horizon whichever way she looked—low, pinkish folds that looked as arid as the vast expanse of desert that she traversed alone.

The sensation of loneliness was intense. Her soul seemed to have shriveled and become too small to contain feelings of warmth and humanity. Fears of eternal solitude preyed upon her, so that she longed and cried out for a voice to remind her that she was not the last person in the universe.

However hard she tried, she could no longer remember where she had been or what she was doing before she began her journey over this parched, glowing landscape. The color of the purple sky hurt her eyes, so that they itched for the sight of cool green or ice blue. There was only the sense of having been abandoned in this stark desolation and a growing impression that she was trying to find something, or someone.

An image of roses hung before her eyes, a trail of roses that moved and vanished like a pale meteor, leaving a brief, faint scent. She became aware of a heaviness upon her hand and saw that her middle finger was encircled by a ring whose large stone echoed the colors of the place in which she'd found herself. At last she experienced a sensation of familiarity and a cessation of the conviction that she was forever condemned to wander this inhuman waste.

She stared at the ring, beginning to remember what had been wiped from her mind. Turning the stone, the picture in it changed to the dark gray and indigos of the gorge in moonlight, and she was peering upward through the tall trees at the walls of Hallowes to the high, small window that lit her room. The uppermost branches swayed in the breeze so that they scratched at the pane.

Moonbranches, she thought gratefully, reveling in the chill after the dehydrating terror of the desert. Something rustled in the undergrowth, and she became aware that someone was there. As she held her breath, Frances heard the faint sound of breathing. All at once she remembered the wood by the church and the churchyard, where the gravestones leaned tiredly, battered by the sea winds.

"Who's there?" she whispered.

Softly the answer came. "Simon. Simon Hallowes."

"I've been looking for you."

"I called you."

"I know," she said. "I heard."

She saw him now, tall and slender, his eyes moontouched, a mirror image of Martin, and yet Frances knew that she'd never have mistaken him for his brother.

"Why didn't you stay a boy of seven?" she asked.

"No one recalls me as a child. They see Martin and remember that as his twin I would have been his counterpart.

So I grow with him because of our mutual identity. If he lives to be a hundred, so shall I, in limbo. He cheated me of life and I can never forgive him."

She was silent, oppressed by his pain and anger. Then she said, "Was it because of the Luck?"

Simon laughed, and the sound was eerie, bouncing back off the thick-leaved branches in mocking echoes. "The Luck! Yes, it was the ring he coveted as much as Hallowes. He got it, too. You know how he did that. Pushed me into the dark pool and held me down with a branch. Then he buried the Luck to foster the belief that it was lost, but I determined that he shouldn't have the pleasure of owning it. I made him forget the place he buried it in its box. Then the floods last autumn loosened the soil and washed it away from the bank."

"And I—kicked it. Every time I intended to tell my aunt or your mother about the ring, I forgot—"

"I made you. I didn't want Martin to find out, but he did."

The breeze rustled the branches, and it was infinitely strange to be in the gorge in moonlight, talking with a ghost.

For the first time Frances thought of the light in her room. Staring up at the yellow rectangle of her window, she said, "Who's up there?"

"Don't you know?"

"I—suppose it must be myself." She shivered.

"You fell asleep. I called you."

She touched the nearest branch and it felt real. "This doesn't seem like a dream. Am I dreaming?"

He shook his head.

"Then I can give you back the ring?"

"No. Do you think I couldn't have got it a thousand times if that were possible? I must have life to be able to claim it, and Martin took that away."

"Can't you ever get it back?"

"There is one way."

"How?"

Simon had grown terribly pale, and the outline of his body was no longer so clear.

"I could get inside him if he'd stay asleep for long enough. But I have to have time, and he always wakes up in an instant."

"Then he'd have to be unconscious?"

Simon gave a sad, self-mocking laugh. "He's as strong as a horse and so very, very careful. He'd have to be extremely ill or off his guard."

The gorge was growing lighter, and the gray had become infused with green. The moon had vanished and the birds were waking.

"I want to be with my mother again," Simon said, in a voice that was far away. "She grieves for me still. And now there's you—"

"Simon—"

But Simon had gone, and Frances knew he wouldn't return. Then the hardness of the ring was biting into her palm, and the yellow glow of the oil lamp shone on her face. Mary was standing over her with an expression of relief.

"Give me such a turn, you did, Miss Frances! Sleeping like the dead, and with all your clothes on. Dropped off reading them magazines, I shouldn't wonder, and the light still on. There's one of them on the floor. Good job it wasn't Mrs. Crabbe who found you."

"Isn't it."

101

"Brought your washing water." Mary returned the magazine to the table, and while her back was turned, Frances slipped the ring off her finger and pushed it under the pillow. For the first time since she'd awakened, she realized that she had no recollection of eating supper last night, though she felt she must have; otherwise her aunt would have sent someone to fetch her.

Somewhere between the desert and the gorge, she had appeared in Aunt Bessie's sitting room and eaten fish or mutton and stodgy pudding, and then returned to her room. No doubt she and her aunt had made conversation, but she could recount no word of it. The thought was frightening. Ghosts seemed stronger than reality.

"Have to go now," Mary said. "You sure you're all right?"

"Yes, thank you. Do you happen to know what we had to eat last night?"

"Well, your aunt had a visit from her friend, Miss Cartwright, and she sent yours up on a tray as she thought you might be bored, since Miss Cartwright's ever so old and rather complaining. But Jenny brought it back to the kitchen, because you called out that you weren't hungry when she knocked."

"No wonder I couldn't remember. I must just have been dozing off. Oh, well, I'll make up for it now. I feel as if I haven't eaten for a week, and I could drink a river dry."

"Makes you sound more like a horse, Miss Frances."

"Doesn't it!" They smiled at one another, and Mary went off, humming tunelessly, her feet heavy on the narrow stairs.

Frances began to wash her face and hands and brush her mussed hair, then decided she must change out of the crumpled blouse and skirt. Her print dress felt too small, as though she'd grown more that she'd imagined since last summer. It

102

had fit her then, but now it was short and tight around the bodice. Still, it would have to do.

Just as she was leaving, she remembered the ring. One of the maids might find it under the pillow. As a temporary measure she pushed it to the back of the top of the wardrobe, lodging it securely into the corner of the band of mahogany that decorated the edge. Even standing on a chair and peering hard, she failed to make out anything more definite than a small shadow. Satisfied, Frances went down to breakfast.

Aunt Bessie expressed surprise at the sight of the change of clothing.

"I wanted to wash my blouse and press the skirt," Frances told her. "The collar and cuffs are a little soiled."

"You can do that in the nursery kitchen. Mary will bring you some water after you've eaten, and there's a pulley for drying. The skirt had better be done down here. It will need the iron."

"I could do them myself when the blouse is dry. I'm used to doing my own laundry at home."

"Of course. I'd forgotten, your poor Mama—"

"I do wish Papa would write. I wonder if he's had any of my letters yet." Frances's fears for her father resurfaced.

"Your Papa will have more to do than write letters."

"I suppose he will." Oddly, the food no longer looked so appetizing. It seemed that Aunt Bessie noticed the shadow that had fallen over her niece's face, for she said gruffly, "It don't do to fret too much. It's not to say that there's ought wrong. There's bound to be delays."

Frances, clutching at straws of comfort, agreed and ate her porridge and egg with a little more enthusiasm. But her heart was sore, and she longed for some tangible sign of Papa's well-being. Her father had been that sort of patriot most easily swayed by recruitment campaigns, and those posters of General Kitchener had done the rest. Those fierce black eyes and his accusing finger made men feel guilty. And there were women with white feathers who lay in wait for youngish, healthy-looking men not in uniform. It was plain that such men were considered too cowardly to fight.

Aunt Bessie, aware of her niece's silence, said, "No news is good news."

"I'm sure you're right."

"Why don't you paint one of them nice pictures this morning? With the family away, you could sit anywhere in the garden."

To Frances, for whom the rest of the day suddenly seemed to stretch away in uneasy misery, the idea was appealing. "Yes, I think I will. The light's just right." She smiled at her aunt, sensing the fact that Aunt Bessie was almost as concerned about Papa as she herself was. There were those who became harassed when they were in positions of responsibility and that less attractive side of Aunt Bessie was always more apparent. She must try to remember that there was an underlying kindness the old lady generally managed to conceal. Old attitudes died hard.

Strong sunshine made the interior of the house so light and welcoming this morning that Frances had difficulty, as she climbed the stairs, in believing that she'd actually met and spoken to Simon Hallowes. Always susceptible to atmosphere, perhaps she'd had a vivid dream. But could one keep on having dreams about the same person? Her face grew warm as she remembered the way he'd said, "Now there's you."

Collecting her painting case, she tried to put thoughts of

104

Simon out of her mind, but this determination didn't prevent her from getting the ring from its hiding place and slipping it into the pocket of her dress.

It was glorious in the walled garden. The sound of bees was loud over the honeysuckle trellis and the heavy masses of roses. Frances walked around the paths until she found the flower she wanted to paint, a sublimely lovely old rose so closely packed with swirling petals that it presented a challenge she knew would have been entirely beyond her before she came to this house.

Why hadn't Francesca been with Simon last night? Why?

Forget them both, she told herself with considerable force. So perfect a day came only rarely. From the moment she put brush to paper, she managed to concentrate purely on the line and color, the subtleties of shading so important to the convoluted center of the chosen bloom. Sir Richard had told her that the very oldest of the roses were French, and this surely was one of those.

Frances forgot all sense of time, knowing only that it was warm, that the air was deliciously scented with the perfume of pine and roses, and that there was some miraculous magic in her fingers. Someone whispered, "You must help Simon. You are the only one who can."

Dropping her brush onto the flower bed, Frances stared around her. There was no one else in the walled garden. Yet the whispered words had been quite clear, as though the person who'd spoken them was sitting on this bench. She moved her hand, encountering nothing tangible. Yet unless she was going mad, someone had ordered her to help Simon. It must be Francesca, drawn to the place where she herself had painted when she was much the same age.

"Francesca?"

There was no sound but the slight rustle of leaves and the hum of bees—only a lingering trace of sadness hanging on the air. Frances got up and washed her brush. If Simon really existed in that strange limbo, she wanted desperately to help him. The thought of the dark pool haunted her, filling her with a great fear and rage against Martin. Had he really known what he was doing? Of course he had. The knowledge lay over her heart like a black stone. Remembering his threats against poor Mary, Frances decided that Martin had always known how to gain his own ends.

The voice had distracted her from her urgency to paint, and she sat for a time, aware of the heat of the sun on her skin and the lazy, soporific drone of insects. She never knew how much time had passed before a man's voice broke into her feelings of belonging to this garden.

Frances blinked and stared into the warm haze. "Mr. Kennedy! What a surprise."

Mr. Kennedy looked at the painted rose. "My dear child, that's perfect. It was a great favorite in the gardens at Versailles. I see now what Sir Richard meant when he said your style was like that of his little ancestress."

"The Halloweses are away."

"So I'm told, but I have permission to come this way at any time. That gate over there leads to the north and south woods, and to the shore and church. Did you find out what you wanted to know? About Francesca Hallowes?"

"Not as much as I'd like."

"That's all one can know. Those laconic entries." Mr. Kennedy looked a little sad. "But they can harrow one, there's no denying it. It's what they leave unsaid."

"Like all the grief and pain. All those lost children—"

"Yes, child." He sat down at the other end of the seat and contemplated the dust on his boots. "But there's also joy."

"Mr. Kennedy, do you—believe in ghosts?"

The minister took time to consider. "Hallowes is an old house, and its walls have heard many things. Atmospheres can hang about a place, echoes from the past, some stronger than others. I'd lie if I said that I've never been aware of something not of this earth."

They sat in the bee-hung garden for a minute or so, then Mr. Kennedy said, "What made you ask?"

Frances couldn't explain without giving the impression that she was perhaps, to put it kindly, a little unhinged, so she contented herself with agreeing that there was an uncanny feel about the place, especially in the attics, to which, owing to Lady Hallowes's kindness, she had access.

"Always the most haunted part of a house, more so even than the cellars," the minister commented, then rose to his feet. "I've just come from the village. It's a case of the return of the warrior. Willie McKenzie's back from the front. Recuperating after being wounded."

Frances's heart thumped painfully. "His family must be relieved to see him."

"There's only his mother. Willie's a confirmed bachelor."

"She must be glad."

Mr. Kennedy stared at her, suddenly remembering her father, unable to think of any word of comfort. It seemed that Willie McKenzie's return was a mixed blessing. Wounded, Frances thought, and knew that they wouldn't have sent Willie home for a mere scratch.

The minister was finding it difficult to lighten the conversation, and Frances couldn't bear to ask the obvious question. Standing up purposefully, she began to pack her painting things, emptying her water jar on a patch of earth between the roses.

"I must go," Mr. Kennedy said, "but my wife still hopes you'll call at the manse again before long. She has a sympathetic ear."

"I will—soon." Frances watched the dark, stocky figure advance upon the side gate and disappear from view. Then, urgently, she seized the case of paints and the still-wet picture and almost ran to the kitchen door to climb the stairs to her room, pull a comb through her hair and cover it with her straw hat, then take her purse from the drawer beside her bed.

She saw no one on her way down the drive. Two blue butterflies hovered over a hydrangea of enormous size, then settled on its large hyacinth-colored blooms. The dark pool lay black and still under the righthand side of the bridge, and Frances hurried past its brooding threat.

Two small boys passed her on the outskirts of the village, staring at her curiously without forgetting a single word of the song they sang in rough, young, fluting voices:

"The bells of hell go ting-a-ling-a-ling,
    For you but not for me.
    The angels they sing ting-a-ling-a-ling
    They hold the goods for me.
    O death, where is thy sting-a-ling-a-ling
    O grave, thy victory?
    The bells of hell go ting-a-ling-a-ling
    For you but not for me."

As soon as they'd finished, they started all over again,

their voices getting fainter and fainter, then dying out on the final chorus. "The bells of hell go ting-a-ling-a-ling/For you but not for me. For you but not for me."

For you but not for me—me—

Almost unseeingly, Frances reached the first of the low white cottages of the village, her eyes fixed straight ahead to where a figure in a wheelchair held court over a mixed group of elderly and quite young people, who listened avidly as he spoke. Everyone fell silent as she approached. Wasn't she not only a stranger, but a girl? But she simply had to hear something of what Willie McKenzie had to say about the war, so she passed the little crowd and entered the grocer's shop, which was cool and dark and mercifully empty.

After standing in the quiet for a minute or two, she realized that the shopkeeper was probably one of Willie's riveted audience. The man in the chair was talking again, his voice queerly flat as though he were still in a state of shock. "My mate copped it the same time as I got this. Just crawled out of our stinking bunkers, trod on a couple of rats on the way, eating something you couldn't recognize, squealing as we blundered over them, they'd got bold as brass, the rats. Outside, we all stopped, waiting for orders and listening to Minnies—"

"What's Minnies?"

"Minenwerfers. Funny sort of shell. Invention of the devil. Filled with nails and jagged bits. Anyway, the captain shouted to get down, but it was a bit late for that. I'll never forget my mate's face. Well it wasn't so much his face as what wasn't there any longer. . . ."

Someone coughed in the silence after Willie's voice tailed away. "Best not to think too much about that, Willie. At least you're alive, and they can't send you back."

"Suppose the food wasn't up to much?" someone else asked, to break a silence far too long for comfort.

"Never offer me bully beef again, nor tinned milk, but neither of them was as awful as the water! Tasted of petrol and chlorine. Couldn't stop drinking the well water when I first got back. So sweet and cool . . ."

A woman's voice broke into the renewed quiet. "You'll tire yourself out, Willie. Don't pester him anymore today, the lot of you. I'm taking him home now."

"We didn't mean any harm, Maggie. Look, I'll push him for you. You've enough with that bag o' tatties and what not. Now don't argue, woman."

The wheelchair squeaked slightly as it ground over the path. "So long!" someone called, and the cry was taken up by a dozen voices. "Look after yourself."

"Don't worry!" the woman cried fiercely. "I'll see that he does." There was the hint of a sob in Willie's mother's voice that struck a responsive chord in Frances. Poor Willie, had he lost one leg or two? It wasn't possible to tell, not with that thick tartan rug pulled over his lap.

Lost in a wave of panic and apprehension, Frances became aware of a voice addressing her from the other side of the counter.

"What is it you want?"

Jerked back to reality, she stared about the shop, not seeing anything she wanted. "Have you any Spanish?" she asked, mentioning the first thing that came into her head.

"You'll get that at the sweetie shop."

"Thank you."

Aware of the suppressed irritation in the old woman's voice, Frances was glad to emerge into the daylight. She seemed to have lived right through the war in the space of quarter of an hour, a war that sounded every bit as terrible as the accounts in that awful newspaper Martin had left for her. Cruel Martin . . .

Blindly, Frances clambered down onto the beach and began to retrace her steps, the sea glittering sharp as knives and the sky a great arc of blue enamel. There seemed no softness or gentleness anywhere.

CHAPTER NINE

It wasn't until after a silent supper with Aunt Bessie, as preoccupied as herself since tomorrow was probably the day the Hallowes family returned, that Frances, putting her hand in the pocket of the too-tight dress to get out her handkerchief, felt the inimical hardness of the ring.

She hadn't thought of the Luck since she'd put it there this morning. In the face of Willie's terrible reality, she'd allowed the memory of Simon and Francesca to recede to a far distance, where they'd become mere shadows. Now they began to reassert themselves, taking shape in the recesses of her mind. She recalled Francesca's whisper: "You must help Simon." Perhaps helping Simon would enable her to forget Willie in his pathetic wheelchair, the hoarse misery in his mother's voice.

"I think I'll go to bed early, Aunt Bessie."

"You do look peaky, so maybe it's best. Don't forget you promised to get the mistress's bottle. She'll be counting on its being here."

"I'll be quite well enough to do that." Frances realized with a jolt that Martin too would be back the following evening. Back to discover that the ring was missing, and it wouldn't take him long to apportion the blame. "What sort of bottle is it?" she asked curiously, forcing back a rush of fear at the thought of Martin's return.

"It helps her ladyship to sleep. Hasn't slept properly since that dreadful business over Master Simon."

"I can understand that."

"Mind that you don't drop it or anything," Aunt Bessie admonished, and bustled away to resume her preparations for tomorrow's portentous happenings. She had no other life but to look after the family at Hallowes.

Left to her own devices, Frances went to her room, unable to get Aunt Bessie's words out of her mind. "Helps her ladyship to sleep. To sleep. Sleep . . ."

Then she thought of Simon's words: "If he'd stay asleep for long enough. . . . He's as strong as a horse and so very, very careful. . . . Always wakes up. Always . . ."

What if Martin couldn't wake up?

The thought, once implanted, refused to go away. But how was she to administer a sleeping draught? Would there be instructions on the bottle, or wasn't it necessary after so many years to remind Lady Hallowes about the proper dosage? Appalled at the thought of making some sort of mistake, Frances tried to forget the notion, but the thought of Simon in perpetual limbo became stronger than her revulsion. She couldn't dismiss Simon as a figment of her imagination, having experienced his warmth and the strengthening bond between them.

Martin began to loom large in her mind. Only a few

more hours and he'd be on his way. The anticipation of his anger frightened her as nothing had before, not even the reality of her father faced with No Man's Land and Willie's Minenwerfers.

She could replace the ring. But that would be cowardly! Only by retaining it could she help Simon, for once Martin had it back, he might well be able to direct matters to his own advantage.

Frances went to the table and began to look through the GOPs. The miscellaneous column was interesting, if only because of the reticence of the questioners in signing themselves: A Sorrowing Wife, E.G. (Leeds), Minnie M., *une jeune fille*, Violet, Myrtle, Hezekiah. Hezekiah stood out like a sore finger, and Frances felt quite sorry for him, having been forced to confide a problem to a girl's paper. But perhaps, like the Brontë sisters, who on occasion had written under masculine pseudonyms, Hezekiah was a girl like herself.

She turned to an advertisement for a "rational" corset bodice, said to be especially useful for growing girls and young ladies. Frances didn't care for the look of it and was glad to set the magazine aside, when she heard the unmistakable sound of Mary's steps on the stairs, followed by a tentative knock at the door.

Frances was pleased to see the little maid, who represented sanity and good-naturedness in a world where suspicion, danger, and darkness seemed to abound. The jug of water Mary brought was welcome, as the air had turned muggy and thundery, and the branches outside the window moved in the heat of the air currents. Frances washed herself gratefully while Mary giggled over the "rational" corset and oohed over a picture of an angelic-looking girl in a lace-trimmed gown, standing with downcast eyes in front of a dark young man who bore an uncannily strong resemblance to Martin Hallowes. "She's pretty as a picture, and isn't he like the young master! Better not show this to Jenny. Got a crush on him, she has, and she'd only imagine this picture's meant to be her and him."

"She's a fool," Frances said, before she could help herself.

"That's not like you," Mary said. "Did seeing Willie upset you?"

"Yes."

"I'll still say prayers for your papa, honest I will."

"Thank you." Frances dried herself and sat in front of the mirror so that Mary could brush her loosened hair. Her image in the shadowy mirror seemed to alter, and the face that looked back at her was that of Francesca. Mary, looking over Frances's shoulder, seemed to notice nothing amiss, but the sensation of being dressed in other clothing, of being caught up in another age, was as strong as the sweet, powdery scent that invaded Frances's nostrils. There had been a scent in the past that could well have smelled like this: patchouli. Again, the thought was transferred to Frances's head: You must help Simon. You must!

Frances shifted uneasily. Surely Mary had heard this? She wasn't entirely unaware of Francesca. There had been the time she'd mentioned the white gown and the long hair. But tonight Mary was not in tune with other worlds and other forces.

"Is that enough brushing, Miss Frances?"

"That's fine, thank you. Very soothing. When I'm rich, I'll have you to look after me, and I'll want to travel the world and you'll go, too, to Paris and Vienna and Rome and Amsterdam, to China and Japan. Africa—"

"Oh, I couldn't go there, miss! Dangerous it is, what with tigers and crocodiles."

"Then we'll go to Florence instead. And Venice—"

"And how are you to make all this money?" Mary inquired, picking up the empty jug.

"I'll paint and sell my pictures when I'm famous."

"It *is* a nice thought," Mary said a little wistfully, as though she recognized all too well the futility of such daydreaming. "Is that the latest one?" She went over to the chest, where the painting of the French rose lay, and stood staring.

"I've seen this one before. Down in his lordship's study, when I do the fires. It's the same!"

"It can't be."

"Looks the same."

"There was a girl once, a Hallowes who painted. Sir Richard said our styles were similar. She liked roses."

"I'd *swear!*" Mary said, unconvinced. "I'll look tomorrow when I lay the fire."

Frances laughed. "Perhaps I *will* be able to make a good living after all, and we'll end up in strange lands."

Mary shuddered. "But not Africa!"

"All right. Not there, I promise. Good-night, Mary."

It was especially quiet once the sound of footsteps died away. Frances sat down to continue her reading, but her thoughts kept wandering to tomorrow. She'd go to the pharmacist's in the village after breakfast, so that there'd be plenty of time to decide upon the next step. It was better not to dwell too much on the thought of tampering with Lady Hallowes's sleeping draught.

116

Tired now, she put on her nightgown, blew out the candle, and got into bed. The twigs outside scratched at the glass, and lifting herself up onto her elbow, she could see the moon, enormous and pale, almost filling the pane.

Moonbranches, she thought, and sank back to fall almost instantly and dreamlessly asleep.

Mary brought Frances her morning washing water in a state of great excitement. "I laid the master's fire," she said, "and that picture's the image of the one in the study. I couldn't see no difference."

"There must have been."

Mary shook her head decidedly. "Not a scrap. Same size. Same colors and shapes. What a funny thing."

"It certainly does seem odd. But you'd have to see them side by side to be certain, and I doubt whether that would ever be possible."

"Make no mistake," Mary insisted. "The master's very particular, specially about what he hangs on his own walls. He'd never countenance rubbish."

Frances laughed. "At least I'll always have one champion."

"I'm sure your papa is!"

Her smile vanished. "Oh, he's very supportive," Frances agreed quietly.

"Sorry if I touched a sore spot. I'm that clumsy." Poor Mary looked contrite.

"I like you the way you are."

"Did you sleep? I wondered after you'd seen Willie, if you'd lie awake thinking. Worrying—"

"I didn't even dream after my head touched the pillow."

"You look better this morning. Ooh, I must go. Crabby—

I mean, Mrs. Crabbe'll be after my blood if I dilly-dally today of all days." And off she went, humming "Early One Morning" until she was out of earshot.

It was odd that Frances hadn't had either dreams or nightmares. If ever there was an occasion on which she'd expected the latter, it was last night, but it was just as though she'd fallen into a deep, dark place like the old Hallowes ice pit, no longer in use, which still yawned horrifyingly behind a rusted grille on the way to the gorge. She'd dropped a small stone through the bars yesterday on her way back from the village, and though there'd been a hollow thud as it struck the wall and bounced off again, she'd never heard it reach the bottom. Aunt Bessie had told her that the ice came in container ships all the way from Canada and Newfoundland.

Going down to breakfast, Frances experienced a tightening of her stomach muscles. Martin was coming. Only a few hours and he'd be there, running up to his room and looking at his egg collection. Confronting her—She shuddered.

"You've gone all white, child," Aunt Bessie said rather crossly, obviously dreading the thought of her day being complicated by illness on top of everything else.

"I'm fine, honestly," Frances told her, making a mental vow to look for some more of the St. John's Wort. If only the pieces she'd sent kept Papa safe! Papa in those awful trenches. The war had become very real since she'd seen Willie. "Is there anything the Halloweses like? Anything I could afford, that is? I must give them something else before I leave."

Aunt Bessie thought ponderously. "Well, there's tea. Ever so fond of Earl Haig, her ladyship is, *and* the master."

"Oh, that's a relief. A tin of tea wouldn't ruin me, though

it doesn't seem much, not for what they're doing. There can't be many like me, invited to such a place."

"And don't you go forgetting it."

Aunt Bessie didn't trust her, Frances thought ruefully. Yet why should she? Hadn't she been enmeshed in deceit ever since she'd come, and now busily contemplating something far worse?

It was a relief eventually to be free to go to the village. Frances kept the ring in her pocket in the meantime, though she'd have to find another place for it before this evening. She'd emptied the last of her small bottle of eau de cologne and rinsed it until it no longer smelled so strongly of the toilet water. It had been impossible to eradicate the scent completely. The bottle was now in her other pocket, creating a little bulge she felt must be apparent to everybody, so strong was her sense of guilt.

The breeze of yesterday had gone, and the air this morning was still and heavy. Muggy weather, Aunt Bessie called it, and told Frances to take an umbrella and not to forget the basket. Thus equipped, she set off, meeting Mary crossing the hall with her wooden box of black-leading materials for cleaning the grates and oven. "Hope you don't get wet, miss."

Frances flourished the umbrella. "Don't work *too* hard."

"Mrs. C's on the warpath, I'm afraid."

"I'd better not hinder you, then. But first, just as a matter of curiosity, what does Master Martin like to drink? I'm going to buy some Earl Haig for his parents, but I doubt if he'd find tea very exciting."

"Oh, it's ginger beer that's Martin's favorite. Always drinking that, he is! Usually keeps a bottle or two in his room."

"And I must get something for Mrs. Kennedy. She was

119

kind, giving me all those magazines. I'll pass them on to the staff before I return them." Frances's heartbeats had quickened, and her voice was breathless. Ginger beer had a strong taste.

"I'm sure the girls would appreciate that. I can just see Jenny in one of them corsets!"

Mary hurried off, still chuckling, and Frances went out to stare at the brooding sky, then started off resolutely down the drive. She passed the postman and thought of asking him whether there was anything for herself, but he looked rather cross and she decided against it.

She averted her eyes from the pool, hurrying over the bridge, her footsteps echoing hollowly against the stone.

She could smell the sea long before she saw it, a rank, rotten smell hanging over the village like a noxious cloud. A dog ran out of an open gateway, barking at her and baring yellow teeth. Frances almost ran to get away from its snapping jaws.

There were few people to be seen, probably because of the pervasive odor of the stinking seaweed that sprawled all along the tideline. Chimneys smoked in spite of the heat, as though the acrid smell of peat was preferable to that of the tangle.

The bell on the pharmacist's door tinkled brassily. Frances stood in the gloom, watching the shifting jewel colors in the large bottles until the old man shuffled behind the counter to stare curiously at her.

"I've come for Lady Hallowes's medicine."

"Oh, aye, you're the lassie staying there for the summer. I could hardly see you."

"The sky's very dark."

"It feels like thunder."

"Yes, it does."

"Wait a minute, lass. The stuff's arrived. I'll get it from the back room."

In town, the pharmacist would have called it his dispensary. What did it matter? A rose by any other name would smell as sweet. For a fleeting second Frances could have sworn she had smelled the perfume of one of those old spiral-petaled roses from France.

The old man came back with the wrapped bottle tied neatly at the neck with a piece of red string. "I can't find the sealing wax, but I know you'll be careful with it."

"Oh, I will," Frances acquiesced gratefully, swamped with relief that the bottle and its contents were accessible.

"Don't suppose you've much to interest you in a hole-in-the-corner place like this," the old man said.

"It's been very—interesting." Frances had difficulty in quelling a note of hysteria in her voice. "Honestly, it has." And she left quickly before she disgraced herself by laughing. It wasn't honest-to-goodness amusement that struggled to escape, but a strange, harsh, derisive emotion that shamed her. Something devil-sent . . .

Looking back at the window, she glimpsed the old man's shadow behind the three tall bottles. It was as if he'd sensed the oddness in her, and she hurried on over the narrow pavement, her skirt swishing the cramped cottage walls, till she reached the grocer's. The woman there did have a tin of Earl Haig tea in the back regions, and while she fetched it Frances looked about for ginger beer. There was a case under the end of the counter with only two stone bottles, and she took out both before anyone else could come in to claim them. It seemed safer to have one extra in case of accidents.

The tin of tea and the ginger beer cost more than she'd expected, leaving her with too little change to buy more than a small quantity of Spanish at the sweet shop.

Staring up at the sky as she started back, she saw that it was almost as dark as prunes over Hallowes.

There was a strange tingling feeling that presaged the thunder the old pharmacist had predicted. Even as she hurried into the gates of the long drive, there was a low, distant rumble that set her feet moving even faster. Stumbling, an incipient stitch in her side, she clattered over the bridge.

Ligthning flashed blue, seeming to plunge into the gorge beyond the black pool. A few raindrops fell heavily, thudding against the dry earth. By the time Frances huddled breathlessly against the door to the side porch, it was raining hard, the sound like countless drumbeats.

Entering, she closed the door quietly, tiptoeing to the nursery stairs and climbing soundlessly toward her room. Pulling off her straw boater she flung it onto the bed. Then she stood one of the stone bottles on the table and began to examine the string-tied parcel. Very carefully, she untied the knots to loosen the paper around the neck of the medicine bottle. She could see it now, the ridged blue glass neatly corked and bearing a white label.

Tincture of laudanum, then the required number of drops. To be used as directed. Frances drew a deep breath. She hadn't expected the dosage to be in drops. Teaspoonsful would have been so much simpler. She took the blue bottle to the window and took out the cork. Tilting it, she emptied a little into the eau-de-cologne bottle, then replaced the cork. Returning it to the hardly disturbed wrappings, she refolded the paper around the neck of the medicine bottle and tied the string exactly as the old man had done. No one would be able to tell that it had been tampered with. Frances was fiercely glad that her fingers were so neat and that her hands hadn't trembled, creasing the paper.

Pushing the stopper into her scent bottle, she thrust it under her pillow and went downstairs with Lady Hallowes's sleeping draught, meeting Aunt Bessie in the passage that led to the kitchens.

"I'm just back. I thought I'd better give you this straightaway."

Aunt Bessie took it, saying with a kind of astonishment, "I thought you'd be half-drowned!"

"I had the umbrella," Frances told her, thinking she must remember to wet it thoroughly when she got back upstairs, then wishing with a curious, sick shame that she was not obliged to pretend.

"Mr. Fraser usually seals this." Aunt Bessie looked suspicious.

"He said he'd run out of sealing wax."

"A good job he didn't give this to anyone less careful. Poison, this is, if you take too much. Lady Hallowes has a special dropper."

"Poisonous? I never thought about its being so dangerous."

"I'd best put it where her ladyship usually keeps it. Now don't be late for lunch, not today when everything is in a rush."

"I won't!"

Upstairs again, Frances wished Aunt Bessie hadn't said what she had about poison. But she hadn't taken more than it said on the label, she'd swear to that. All that would happen was that Martin would fall asleep so that Simon might have his chance to live. She would do anything for Simon. Anything at all. He deserved a second chance.

Frances heard the rumble of approaching wheels and her stomach muscles clenched involuntarily. Mary had just left her to join the others in the servants' quarters in the attic, and she felt terribly alone.

Not daring to wear the ring on her hand, she had slipped it onto a chain that had belonged to her mother, showing the locket it normally carried at the front, the ring tied at the back so that it wouldn't shift and tucked inside the close-fitting neck of her blouse.

It was dusk now, and the moon rode high and mistletoe colored in a pewter sky, outlining the black branches. The Halloweses were so late that Aunt Bessie had told the girls, apart from Jenny, to go to bed. The fires were on in the dining room and drawing room, and a cold supper was already prepared, the beds turned down. Jenny would clear away and take hot water upstairs. The maids took turns doing late duty when the master and mistress were delayed.

Frances went silently down her little staircase and listened to their voices when they arrived, hearing only disjointed fragments of sentences. "Such an uplifting service—baby didn't behave—tears—Martin—so tall now—difficult to fit him— we'll retire—soon as supper's over—thank you for staying up. Frances—" Then the door closed and there was silence.

Ears tingling at the mention of her name, Frances withdrew. Why had Lady Hallowes spoken about her?

Then she remembered the sleeping draught, and her

heart was heavy with guilt. Pacing the room, she wondered how long they would take to eat the cold game pie and gooseberry tart, then return to the lower floor.

Perhaps Martin wouldn't look in the egg case tonight; or maybe he'd look through the glass top and think it hadn't been touched. But he was sufficiently devious to realize that others could behave like himself under sufficient duress. Yet when he discovered—if he discovered—his loss, wouldn't he first suspect Jenny, who'd seen him beside the egg collection? She'd said how angry he was at her intrusion, how he'd thrust her out of his bedchamber. How he'd glared at her.

Some of the tension left Frances's body. He'd certainly think first of Jenny, who had access to his room and whose suspicions obviously had been aroused. But there was no way in which he could question her this evening, was there? Oh, but he could! Jenny would be taking around the hot water, since it was her turn to do late duty. Perhaps Lady Hallowes would go upstairs first. Martin couldn't shout and rage at Jenny with his mother just along the hall.

Someone was coming up the staircase to the first floor. Frances recognized the timbre of Lady Hallowes's voice, high-pitched and a little reedy, like the tap music from the nursery.

Sir Richard murmured a reply, then said more loudly, "Don't stay up reading, Martin. You'll only be bad-tempered in the morning." A door closed, and then a second, defiantly loud. Master Martin was already in an ill humor, and Frances flinched from the threat.

She heard Jenny knock quietly with the first of the hot-water jugs, then patter away for the second. A lifetime seemed to pass before the girl returned to knock on the second door. This time there was no sound of departing footsteps; neither could Frances hear any upraised voice. But there were furies other than noisy ones.

Perhaps Martin hadn't yet found out and was merely enjoying Jenny's company, because she was pretty and such visits would be more than frowned upon.

Frances froze. Someone was passing the foot of the stair, and whoever it was was weeping very softly. The slim, dark shadow cast briefly on the wall was Jenny's. So Martin had been coldly angry, taxing the girl with theft. Soon it would be her own turn. But there was nowhere to go to escape, and since the encounter could not be avoided, Frances returned upstairs slowly, willing herself to be brave. Martin would find her a tougher adversary than a boy of seven.

She got out more of *The Girl's Own Papers* and sat at the small table with as much composure as she could muster. Mary had brushed her hair as usual, and it fell over her shoulders, warming them like a small cloak. She forced herself to read a story, reflecting that without the hammer blows of piety that reduced it to little more than a religious tract, it could have been far more exciting, and that a leaven of humor would have improved it enormously.

Slowly, she realized that her back felt icily cold in spite of the mantle of hair. Frances shivered, her face paling.

"Good evening, Frances," Martin said quietly.

She rose so quickly that her chair overturned. Though she had expected him to come, and had prepared herself for the visit, now that he was here she felt a swift uprising of panic. But she mustn't show it! Forcing herself to frown, she said, "Must you creep about so quietly? Couldn't whatever it is have kept until morning?" Then she bent to pick up the chair.

"It couldn't keep till then."

Again she forced her features into a look of surprise. "I don't think your parents would care to find you here at this hour."

"Where is it?"

"Oh, dear, this is all too subtle for me. Where is what?"

"The ring," he ground out savagely. "As if you didn't know."

"What are you talking about? You took that long ago." She injected just the right amount of surprise and annoyance into her voice.

"I think you've got it."

"How would I know where to look? I'm not a magician."

Martin stared around the room, then at the chain that glinted against the front of her blouse, his gaze focusing on the locket. He moved forward to examine it more closely. Too late, Frances remembered that she hadn't searched for fresh St. John's Wort. Her parents must protect her. Before he could touch it, she snapped open the locket to show him the pictured faces of her mother and father.

"This was Mama's locket, and I won't allow you to touch it. If you do, I'll scream loud enough to rouse the entire household."

"Who said I was going to? What a fuss." Martin withdrew his outstretched fingers and returned to his surveillance of the sparsely furnished room.

"You are at liberty to search it," Frances told him coldly, though her heart thudded like a drum.

"That only indicates that I shan't find it."

"Take it as you will. Now, I'm tired, Martin, and I would prefer it if you left."

Their eyes met, and she was terribly conscious of something dark and old and wicked behind his gaze. He smiled, showing sharp white teeth. "Not quite the white mouse who arrived, are you? Not so innocent."

She flushed. He made innocence sound so paltry.

"We all must grow up."

"How profound," he mocked, but she noted the underlying anger and uncertainty. Martin wasn't sure of anything. He might think Jenny had lied. Girls like Jenny always cried when they were in tight corners. He'd interrogate Jenny again before he turned the full force of his displeasure on herself. The thought of that displeasure filled her with dread.

"Good-night."

He moved away, still grinning, only stopping for a moment in the doorway to look back and say, "I *will* get it back, you know, and whoever has it is a thief. The Luck is—"

"Still your father's," Frances retorted. "I can't think why you didn't give it to him. I think that's what he would wonder—"

The smile disappeared, leaving an expression of black ferocity that struck her dumb. Then he went, not forgetting, even in his frustration, to tread softly.

She closed the door and leaned on it, pushing down the inclination to gasp, to cry out. By this time tomorrow he'd have reassured himself about Jenny's innocence, and all his suspicions would be centered upon herself. Think about Simon, Frances told herself, and went on concentrating on Martin's brother until she was calm enough to think about getting ready for bed.

CHAPTER TEN

Sir Richard, who obviously had had a trying time with Martin for the past few days, had insisted upon his son's remaining in his room to prepare some work for the coming school term.

He'd looked in at Aunt Bessie's little sitting room as she and Frances breakfasted in a not-too-companionable silence, and said that Martin was to have no distractions from any member of the staff but Mrs. Crabbe.

Frances received the distinct impression that Sir Richard had been aware of Jenny's prolonged visit last night, and that Martin had this morning been taxed with that knowledge.

"I'll take his lunch and tea myself," Aunt Bessie assured her master.

"Boys become a handful at a certain age," he said ruefully. "I've tried to make allowances, heaven knows, but—" He shrugged and looked as close to anger as he could ever be. "Sometimes I wish we'd been blessed with a daughter. Someone like Frances." And he smiled kindly.

"Oh, Frances has her own prickliness," Aunt Bessie said

very positively, and Sir Richard laughed and went away.

"Poor man," Aunt Bessie sympathized. "It makes a body wonder how the other lad would have turned out."

Frances wanted to spring to Simon's defense but forced herself to remain silent. It would be prudent not to show too great an interest in Martin's twin. Then, thinking of Martin's incarceration, a load was lifted from her heart and mind. Master Hallowes would be far too occupied to do anything about the ring today, and the sense of freedom that gave her was a joy.

"Could I take some sandwiches and stay out all day? It's so lovely outside and you wouldn't have to bother about my lunch as well as Martin's."

"Master Martin to you, young lady! But I don't see why not—only you wouldn't be getting into mischief or snagging your skirt again?"

"I'll be careful."

"Go and put your outdoors on, then, and come to the kitchen on your way out."

Frances ran upstairs to get her purse and basket and to change into her comfortable boots. She had the ring tied onto her gold chain and had, last night, emptied the laudanum into one of the ginger beer bottles, marking the label with a black dot so that she'd know which was which if anyone moved them in her absence.

There was nothing she had to do, nothing she must remember, and the day she'd dreaded became a time of promise.

The bundle of sandwiches, fruitcake, and apple was ready when she went to the kitchen. Mary, busy in the scullery with a heap of vegetables for the broth, smiled and went on with her uninspiring task. Frances wished that Mary might have come with her but knew better than to voice the thought. All that was required of herself was to keep out of Aunt Bessie's way and not to annoy her hosts or to give the servants ideas above their station.

Once outside, with the sun shining and the insects filling the air with their sleepy humming, Frances walked around the house, trying to decide on a plan of action.

Something made her look up at the windows of the principal bedrooms. It was a mistake. Martin glowered down at her, his lips pressed into a hard, unforgiving line.

Frances hurried past as though from a charging bull. The force of Martin's gaze was almost as bad as the feel of horns tearing through the flesh of her shoulders. She ran between the trees, missing the start of the drive, knowing only that she must escape.

She became aware that she was on what appeared to be a bridle path that must run closely parallel to the drive, yet far enough away from it to leave the main road quite invisible. There was an odd comfort in being unseen, sheltered by the trees. Stabs of sunlight fell upon the track, periodically covering her in a cloak of dappled whiteness. The sound of her heart was like horses' hooves thudding against the earth. If she closed her eyes she could almost feel that she *was* on a horse's back, galloping here as many Halloweses had done before her.

She came to the stream, obviously some distance from the pool. Here there was no need for a bridge. The water ran shallowly, sliding over and around a rocky bed, the ford marked by tall stepping-stones. There were seven of them, worn by the constant presence of the stream, dried today by the sun and the breeze.

131

Frances walked from one to another, charmed by the clearness of the water and the sight of dragonflies, preferring this route to the village. She hadn't meant to return to the village so soon. But it was still early in the day, and consequently she could go further afield after visiting the shops.

Noticing the yellow flowers of St. John's Wort, she picked some, placing the sprigs carefully in her basket, hoping that her father carried his close to his heart. One could live without arms and legs, but a heart or a head was much too vulnerable. She tried not to think of Papa, but it wasn't easy to dismiss him from her mind. Then the warm sunshine and the insect hum again enveloped her, so that even Martin's cold dislike and wickedness and Papa's danger receded into an indolent peace.

The tide was high as she emerged from the end of the trail to find herself at the far side of the village. Ahead there were clusters of black, eroded rocks as high as a house, sinister and brooding, etched with pale orange lichen.

Dwarfed by their size and awed by their strange, twisted shapes, Frances stared. Beyond their darkness were sharp glimpses of blue sea and folds of paler blue hills beyond the point where the cliffs ended. Gulls swooped, crying discordantly over some unseen treasure on the narrow beach that was all that remained uncovered by the tide and overlaid with pebbles and large, smooth rocks.

She made her way through the cold canyons between the worn formations, shivering at the contrast between these windy crevasses and the balmy pleasures of the bridle path. Far away, a train sounded mournfully. Trains were sad things that took people away, sometimes forever. Oppressed by the savage splendor of the rocky maze, Frances worked her way around the last of the huge stones and scrambled onto the narrow path that edged the beach.

A cottage lay not far away, its chimney smoking sullenly, a few spindly apple trees showing beyond a fence with half its palings gone. No living thing showed itself, and Frances was tired from her exertions. Placing her jacket on a patch of wiry grass around which campions danced in the air current, she opened the packet of sandwiches and took a bite from the first, enjoying the tang of fresh cheese with a touch of sharpness. Another sandwich contained neat rounds of hard-boiled egg; still another, honey. She savored the differing flavors and the good taste of the home-baked bread, then ate the apple, deciding to save her piece of cake for later.

The sea was receding inch by inch, uncovering a strip of dark sand. Fastening her hands around her knees, she closed her eyes and listened to the slow crunch of the tide on shingles. Ages later, it seemed, she became aware of a squeaking noise and upraised voices, one pleading, the other angry.

"She's doing no harm," the woman was saying.

"Spying, that's what she's at!"

"Willie, that's wrong and foolish—"

"Why are you there?" Willie McKenzie shouted, and Frances, scrambling to her feet, looked, bewildered, into his distorted face.

"I thought—"

"What did you think?"

"Well, that this was a public path—"

"Aye, it may be for walking along, but *not* to sit at folks' front doors."

"I'm sorry. I meant no harm. I'll go away." Palefaced, Frances began to pick up her scattered possessions.

133

"He doesn't know what he's saying," Mrs. McKenzie said apologetically, replacing the tartan rug that was beginning to slip from Willie's lap.

"Oh, don't bother to put that back. If she wants to see what I've become, let her have a proper look!" And he whipped the rug aside before his mother could stop him.

"Willie!" Mrs. McKenzie said, in a low, strangled voice.

Willie had lost both of his legs just above the knees, and his mother had cut a pair of his trousers to fold neatly under the rounded stumps. Frances gave a small, inarticulate cry and whirled away from him.

"You've been very cruel," the woman said. "That's the lass who's staying at Hallowes. And d'you know why she's there? Because her father's away to the war. She'll have heard of you, no doubt, and I shouldn't wonder but she's sick with worry about him. I'm sorry, lass, and I'm saying so for both of us. I little thought to see the day I'd be ashamed of my own son, poor misguided soul that he is."

"I didn't know you lived here. I won't bother you again." Blindly, Frances began to walk away toward the village.

"Don't go, miss," Mrs. McKenzie called after her. "I'm that sorry. So'll he be when he's had time to think."

"It's all right, Mrs. McKenzie. I understand." But under the wounded feelings Frances didn't really understand. She had a dreadful picture of Papa coming home wounded, hating her and anyone else for encroaching upon his bitterness. It seemed that to the maimed, the whole were monsters to be reviled. Perhaps that was understanding.

Slowly, she began to think of other things, to steep herself in the neglected charm of the small cottages, built low to withstand the prevailing wind. Their tiny windows seemed to

134

hide secrets no one would ever discover. Like Hallowes—

The thought of Hallowes made her intensely aware of Martin, waiting for her with hatred, so she turned her attention to the shops, deciding to take back bull's eyes and stripy mints instead of the cough candy that first attracted her and that was pleasant to eat even when one hadn't a cold. But she suspected that Mary would prefer the others, and she liked to share her treats with a friend.

She bought some stamps at the dark little post office, where an old lady stared curiously at her and whispered behind her hand to a companion. As Frances waited for change, she saw the hard-faced man from Hallowes pass by, his shadow momentarily casting the poky little room into even deeper shadow, another and sharper reminder of Martin and his revenge.

Outside again, she was unable to remember just where the bridle path emerged, and decided she'd better return by the drive, which conveniently was marked by tall pillars of stone with cormorants sitting on them, the wrought-iron gates always left open. Before the Halloweses had come down in the world, there once must have been a tiny gatehouse there, but that no longer existed—only some small remnants of a tumble of gray stone, barely visible behind a rampart of willow herb, the rest taken for building purposes or repairing walls.

The trees of the drive pressed together as if to shut out the sky, leaving her in a cool green tunnel that only opened out as she arrived, panting, at the bridge. The black surface of the pool today held no light. Like some bleak obsidian mirror, it menaced and haunted her. She wondered how Martin felt as he passed this place. Did he feel pity or guilt? Then she reminded herself that she had no real proof that he'd killed his brother. Perhaps she'd dreamed everything under the stress of fearing for her father. Hallucinations? But the fact that the ring that was supposed to be lost in the pool had most certainly been buried in the wood near the church reassured her that she *had* heard the voices of Simon and Francesca and seen them in some strange shift of time. She couldn't be wrong.

Looking at the watch that was pinned to her blouse, she noted that it was still early. That horrible encounter with the McKenzies had driven her homeward before she'd intended, but she hadn't seen the minister and his wife for a few days, and it would be pleasant for a change to be somewhere where she was wanted. Mrs. Kennedy was kind, even seeming genuinely to approve of her.

Instead of going back to the terrace in front of Hallowes, Frances cut across to the beach and walked toward the church. The weathercock swayed, glinting under the sun. Gravestones cast long black shadows over the tufted grass, Francesca's the darkest of all.

Frances shivered and hunched her shoulders, glad to be past the churchyard and into the thicket that hid the manse. Even before she reached the door, she knew that however hard she knocked, there was no one to hear. The Kennedys were about their parochial duties.

Perversely, Frances took the forbidden path, uncaring of the bramble trails and spiky thorns. The day that had started so well had not lived up to her expectations, and she felt hurt and rebellious.

The back of her neck tingled. She remembered the ring secured to the chain. Her skin felt cold, then hot, where the ring rested as though there was something in this part of the wood that triggered off the magic, clairvoyance, whatever it was. Perhaps devilry was a better word?

She hurried, disregarding the pluck and scratch of the twigs. There would be time to attend to the damage before she need see her aunt.

No one saw her enter by the side door or cross the checkered hall. The staircase seemed to grow narrower as she went higher, as though trying to close in upon her, and again she was reminded of *Alice in Wonderland*. Then she was in her room. The sun had shifted and it was dim, the branches seeming thicker and closer to the window than before.

Then she saw the letter. It was propped against a jug in the center of the table. There was only one person who'd send her a letter. To think that it had probably arrived just after she'd gone this morning! And all day, while matters had gone steadily from bad to worse, it had been there, waiting to be read.

She went toward it like a person in a trance.

Afterward, torn between relief and pain, it was difficult to envisage a time without the letter. Papa had received the gift of the St. John's Wort and was carrying it in his breast pocket where he kept his lighter, saying that the lighter would go out of use once his supply of tobacco ran out. The letter was marred by rectangles that cut out various portions, obviously things the censor wished to remain secret, so there was no way of knowing where he was, or indeed, what he was doing. But at least he'd been able to say that she was a good, thoughtful girl, and that she was to take care of herself, and to tell Aunt Bessie that he'd be in touch with her before long, and not to worry, for the devil took care of his own.

137

The back of her neck tingled again, and she knew that Simon wanted to speak to her. Slowly, Frances unfastened the chain and took off the ring, slipping it instead onto her finger.

"Help me," Simon whispered. "You haven't forgotten?"

"I haven't forgotten. I've got something that will make Martin sleep. Some stuff your mother takes in order to forget the shock of losing you."

"Poor Mama."

"It may not be easy to get Martin to drink it, but you must be ready to seize your opportunity. Do you understand?"

The whispering voice was faint. "I understand."

"Where are you, Simon? Why can't I see you?"

But there was only silence and the impression of someone having gone, the only hint of his presence in a shifting blur behind the branches that later would obscure the moon.

Frances replaced the ring onto the chain, refastening the neck of her blouse. Then she went to fetch the two bottles of ginger beer and set them on the table. It wasn't too late to pour the doctored drink down the nursery sink. But why should she? She wasn't doing anything really wicked, only helping a boy whose life had been stolen to change places with the thief.

She sat staring at the small black mark that distinguished the bottle that contained the sleeping draught, looking at it for so long that the spot and all the letters on the label seemed to quiver then turn into hieroglyphics. Her father had retreated into a world far away, and only the bottles and the Hallowes boys seemed starkly real.

Something moved in the depths of the mirror.

Frances got up and faced the door. "Good evening, Martin. I was expecting you."

138

Her composure surprised Martin, and he frowned. "I thought you'd still be out. Crabby said you would be late."

"I changed my mind. I suppose you came to search my room? Go ahead. You won't find much."

He laughed unpleasantly. "We *are* brave this evening."

"Have you just been released from your room? I understand you've been segregated all day."

"Listening at keyholes?" he inquired, and came toward her. "I suppose that since you suggest I look here for the ring, it's somewhere else?"

She nodded. "And I won't tell you where."

His face grew ugly. "You will!" And he picked up her hand, twisting her wrist so painfully that she cried out. "I want that ring and I mean to have it."

"I'll scream if you do that again. You'd have a job to explain that away. I scream very loudly."

"I'll say it was horseplay."

"You're not supposed to be talking to anyone but my aunt."

He was silent, and she knew she'd scored a point. There would be maids in all sorts of places at this time of day who'd hear her scream. Then his gaze fell on the bottles of ginger beer. She snatched up the innocent one and made to grab at the other, but he got there before her.

"Please give me that," she said coldly. "I bought it to give to someone."

"I think I'll keep it. As you are keeping the Luck."

"That's not at all the same thing," she protested.

"I won't give it back."

Frances struggled to keep the triumph from her face and voice. "I hope it chokes you!"

"It's never done that before. Ginger pop's a favorite of mine. I'll enjoy this." Martin held the bottle behind his back.

"Frances?" Aunt Bessie's voice floated up the well of the stair. "Are you there?"

"Yes, I am." Frances called out quite calmly, though her heart was racing wildly. Who could have thought it would be so easy? She couldn't have planned it this way.

"I'm coming up," Aunt Bessie shouted.

Martin slid out of sight in the direction of the nursery, and Frances listened to her aunt's laboring steps, unexpectedly pleased to see the stout, black-clad body and flushed face.

"You got it, then, your pa's letter?"

"Yes. Would you like to read it? He mentions you."

"Indeed, I would." Aunt Bessie lowered herself, creaking, onto a chair and wiped her brow with her handkerchief. "Thought about nothing else all day."

"You should have looked at it. We've no secrets from you." Frances held out the folded paper.

"Oh, that's not right. A person's letter isn't public news. Very private, letters are. Oh, my! Haven't they cut out a lot of it! No address. I suppose they do the same with ours. I expect this was sent before he embarked. Wouldn't want spies to know where that place is. Drop bombs on it, I daresay."

"It'll be a lot longer before I get the next."

Aunt Bessie opened her mouth, then closed it again. Frances guessed that she'd intended to make some cautionary remark, then thought better of it.

"At least I know he's all right," Frances said bravely.

"What's this plant he mentioned?"

"Oh, something that was supposed to protect him. An old wives' tale. I—hoped it still might work."

140

"Prayers might be better."

"Oh, don't worry! I say plenty of those."

"It doesn't do to dabble in witchcraft."

"It's nothing like that. Really."

Aunt Bessie hauled herself out of the chair. "There's your letter, child."

"Thank you. Yours will come soon."

"I can't imagine why your pa had to join up and worry us so much."

"I don't think he did it just to worry someone." Frances folded the letter small and tucked it into her breast pocket. "People can be very unkind, and Papa looked young for his age. Women hand out white feathers instead of calling you a coward to your face."

"Whatever next!"

"Didn't you know? It was in all the newspapers."

"When do I have time to read those!"

"No, I don't suppose you get much opportunity."

"It's almost suppertime. You'd best come down with me now and have it." Aunt Bessie turned to go.

Frances stared around the room, remembering Martin's presence along the hall, then pushed the remaining bottle of ginger beer behind the folds of the curtain. Let Martin think she minded the fact that he'd taken the other sufficiently to hide this one. It would make him all the keener to take the other one down to his bedroom and drink it, if only out of spite.

"Has Master Martin had his?"

"I'm going to take it now."

Frances knew Martin could hear their conversation. As a result he would be far too busy getting back unobserved to spend time prying in her room. She fancied she heard him move.

"Why is he in disgrace?"

"Making too free with those who should know better. Handsome is as handsome does."

"That sounds very mysterious," Frances said innocently, following her aunt around the angle of the staircase.

"Far too great a belief in their own looks, some girls have. Well, it's done them no good in this case. Don't be surprised if there's a change in the domestic staff before the week's out."

"Oh, I do hope Mary isn't involved!"

"Why should she be, you poor goose? Mary may not be a beauty, but she knows her place, not like some. Now I can't say more than that. You go and wait while I attend to Master Martin." And Aunt Bessie went off to the kitchen.

It was quiet in the housekeeper's sitting room, and the plush curtains and bobble-fringed cloth looked heavier and more claustrophobic than ever. Standing at the window, Frances could see into the gorge. There was quite a drop from the bank to the riverbed. The sheer fall fascinated her with its unexpected danger. It hadn't been obvious from her bedroom window, and she realized that her own view had been obscured by leafy branches. Then she was reminded of the ice pit that was far deeper than she'd expected. Hallowes was filled with surprises, not all of them pleasant.

Her aunt returned with a look of grim triumph. "I've seen to that limb of Satan. Scowled at me like a demon, he did, and never a word of thanks. It'll be better with him out of the house, if you ask me."

Just then, Mary appeared with their own supper, and it wasn't necessary to comment on Aunt Bessie's remarks concerning Martin. It was easy to see that she was becoming irritated by the need to serve Martin's meals separately, and his lack of appreciation.

The pot pie was delicious, its pastry decorated with rabbits and browned to perfection, but for Frances it might as well have been sawdust, since she could now think of nothing but Martin's drinking the perhaps lethal ginger beer. What if she'd put in too much?

"You're very quiet," Aunt Bessie said at last, wiping her mouth with her linen napkin and surreptitiously adjusting one of the whalebones in her stays.

"I did walk quite a lot."

"Where did you go?"

Frances recounted her day's proceedings without mentioning the scene outside the McKenzies' cottage. Then, seeing that her aunt, for a change, wanted conversation, she asked her, "Why was I called Frances? It wasn't one of Mama's names, or yours. I've often wondered."

"Oh, there were Franceses way back in our family. My grandmother was a Frances, and her grandmother was Frances Louise. That'd be your great-great-grandmother. But there were quite a few Elizabeths, too, and the odd Margaret. We used to like talking about the old family names."

"Frances Louise?" The name was terribly familiar, but it wasn't for a minute or two that Frances remembered where she'd seen it.

In the register of births at the manse.

Afterward, Frances tried to decide what had made her ask that question, but no answer came. Out of the blue, the words had formed themselves and nothing could ever be quite

143

the same. Frances Louise. It was such an unusual combination, and Francesca's baby hadn't died.

She experienced a strong compulsion to revisit the manse to find out more about the infant.

Martin didn't reappear that evening, and she had awful visions of him lying drugged or dead, so as soon as breakfast was over next morning, she rushed up to her room to get her jacket, seeing that the sky looked overcast. It ocurred to her, as she put on her coat and fetched a clean handkerchief, that her painting of the French roses seemed to have disappeared. Then, deciding that it might have slipped down behind the furniture, she put off a search for it until later. The important thing was to get out of the house.

To her relief, she met no one on the way out and was soon walking along the beach toward the church. The sky was a dark pearl, and there were no contrasts of light and shade. She seemed lost in a gray vacuum. The church had never looked so barred and empty, and there was mist around the gravestones. Here and there a dark fragment of stone showed itself briefly, then was lost.

She forced herself along the encroaching shrubbery to the manse, feeling like Beauty entering the domain of the Beast. No light glinted on the windows, and they, too, like those of the church, gave the place a forlorn, unoccupied look. Yet, unlike yesterday, she sensed that the Kennedys were there.

Mrs. Kennedy answered her knock, seeming pleased to see her, inviting her into the untidy warmth of the kitchen to partake of coffee that was still drinkable.

Mr. Kennedy was there, too, without his collar and looking more like the gardener, but equally friendly, pulling out

144

a chair for her and going for the biscuit tin, which contained the remains of last time's abernethies.

"Lassies can always find a corner for a biscuit," Mrs. Kennedy pronounced comfortably when Frances protested that she'd just had breakfast. "Anyway, it's the time we have a break."

They sipped coffee for a few minutes, exchanging chit-chat. Then Mr. Kennedy ventured, "But you had a reason for calling, didn't you?"

Frances hesitated, then said, "Well, I wanted to see you, of course. You've both been so kind. But I did want to ask about Francesca Hallowes. There was no record of her baby dying, so I wondered if she was brought up by the father?"

There was silence for a moment, then Mrs. Kennedy said, "You're a grown-up lass and I think you can understand. It's obviously important to you. There wasn't any wedding, and the only person who could tell you any more than that would be Sir Richard himself. He naturally has charge of the Halloweses' papers. Is there some special reason you want to know, or is it just a way of passing the time, my dear, because you're left so much on your own?"

Frances was tempted to say that it was the latter, but one didn't lie to the clergy, especially when they showed that they liked you. "It probably seems silly to you, but I do think it's important, though I wouldn't want to bother Sir Richard."

"He probably knows the family history backwards, and he's a good fellow. Not likely to take it amiss. Most likely to be flattered at your interest in the Halloweses. Not the family they once were. Coffers depleted, and that sort of thing. But salt of the earth."

"You could do some of your painting and he'll most likely

come to you of his own accord. I know he's got a high opinion of that. The rose garden. That's where you're most likely to meet," Mrs. Kennedy suggested.

"I expect you're right. I hope he won't take me for a busybody?"

"From what he's said about you, I doubt that," the minister assured her, his blue eyes very kind and reminding her of Papa's.

"Those old photographs, could I look at them again?"

Mrs. Kennedy looked mystified but told Frances that she could. "I thought I was the only one to feel a sort of kinship for those!"

"There was one in particular—"

"Oh, I don't want to pry. You go through to the morning room and have a good inspection. We'll still be here."

Thanking her, Frances went across the hall. Through the open door she could see a sulky fire not yet properly alight, the morning gloom and a patina of damp on the table and old rosewood piano. She stared at the ranks of brown portraits, the stiff bodies and set features. None of these people looked as if they had enjoyed having their photographs taken.

She found the photograph she wanted and looked at it for some time. It was of a well-corseted lady of commanding appearance, and she bore a distinct resemblance to Aunt Bessie. But a lot of older women looked like her. Hadn't she herself noted the fact that her aunt resembled pictures of Queen Victoria, with those heavy-lidded eyes and small chin? But Aunt Bessie's great-grandmother had been called Frances Louise.

Frances's thoughts whirled like the pieces in a snowstorm when one shook it. She'd had a snowstorm once, a little glass

dome with a church inside, but it had been broken accidentally. She still remembered the disappointment she felt as the
water ran out of it, dispelling the illusion of magic.

She became aware that someone was beside her and found
Mr. Kennedy studying the portrait that was so reminiscent of
her aunt.

"I came to see if you were all right. You've been so long."

"I'm fine. They—they look so uncomfortable, don't
they."

"Probably were. If sitters were fidgety, they had their
heads put in clamps to keep them still."

"Oh, dear!" Frances found herself laughing a little too
loudly.

"Come and have some more coffee," the minister suggested. "It's none too warm in here, and you're shivering."

"I do believe I am." She allowed herself to be led back
to the kitchen, her mind darting off at dangerous tangents. If
the portraits were all relations of Mr. Forbes, the previous
minister, perhaps he'd had good reason to seek a post at Hallowes. Family members lost touch with one another during
times of crisis or believed one another bereaved. Addresses
could be lost in fire or flood. Members of the same family
could disapprove of another and disown them, and, once the
bond was broken, it might be impossible to trace the sister or
brother, uncle or aunt, father or cousin. Perhaps one sometimes succeeded.

Could Frances Louise Hallowes be her own ancestor?

The question seemed to burn in her brain. It was considered a disgrace for a girl to have a child without being wed,
probably even more so for a girl from a good family with proud
connections. May Shanks, a girl in her own street at home,

147

had become pregnant, and the baby had been adopted. The place had buzzed with disapproval and harsh remarks, and May had been forced to go to Wales to live with an older married sister. Frances hadn't been supposed to know about the affair, but people didn't always lower their voices, and she did have ears.

Francesca had died, and it was more than probable that her little girl had been adopted and had lived out her life under some other name. Marrying and adopting yet another name. Lost after a generation or two.

That might explain the feeling of having seen the house before, her involvement with Francesca, and the queer business of the paintings.

"My dear, you really are in a brown study!" Mrs. Kennedy chided amiably. "Did you have a bad night?"

"Not really. Sorry if I'm being rude."

"You'd never be that. Too much breeding."

"I'm very ordinary," Frances disclaimed quickly.

"Have it your own way. But Sir Richard wouldn't think so highly of anyone he didn't think deserved his trust and friendship. The Halloweses have always set high standards. Some say too high."

"My dear," Mr. Kennedy said warningly, "it's not for us to say—"

"Oh, I didn't say it, someone else did."

"We are not bound to repeat it." Mr. Kennedy could be oddly impressive when he chose to disapprove, but his wife wasn't easily suppressed. She laughed cheerfully and looked at Frances like a conspirator. "If one can't speak freely inside one's own four walls, there's something wrong somewhere."

Mr. Kennedy frowned. "I'll be in the study if you want me. Good day, Frances."

They stared after him, Mrs. Kennedy shaking her head. "It's funny but it's only the Halloweses who can make him so stuffy. I think they overawe him."

"I wonder if Mr. Forbes felt like that about them?"

"Now I wonder what put that into your head?"

"Didn't I hear that he was a relation of Sir Richard's?"

Frances had heard nothing of the sort, but her desire to test her momentous theory had outgrown caution.

"We never heard of it, but that's not to say it wasn't true. If only those old ancestors could speak, we'd hear a tale or two."

"I must go, I forgot to say where I was going, and Aunt Bessie may be looking for me."

"I daresay you won't be sorry when the summer's over and you're back with all your friends."

But the prospect had no reality. Frances could think of nothing but the present.

"Come back soon!" Mrs. Kennedy called as Frances left.

She waved, saying that she would, and plunged into the tangled shrubbery, which was dim and mysterious under the threat of rain, heavy with mingled scents. It would be good to sit in the rose garden, to paint all the stress and emotion out of herself, but this wasn't the right day. Images began to crowd in her mind of Martin lying very still. But she had taken out the bottle last evening in a kind of revulsion that might have ended in the contents being poured away. He had chosen to take it, but the thought didn't smother her feelings of guilt.

She entered the gardens by the gate the minister used when taking the shortcut. The roses, their colors dimmed by the heavy cloud, swayed gently. She looked at them with Francesca's eyes.

"Good morning, Frances."

Blinking, she saw Sir Richard at the side door, his face betraying a cool displeasure. The ring on the chain gave a warning tingle. Frances braced herself for trouble.

"Good morning."

"Would you come inside? There's something I must ask you."

"Of course," she replied mechanically. So Martin had drunk the ginger beer and his father had found out that it had been tampered with. Lady Hallowes would have remembered the unsealed bottle that contained laudanum.

Frances followed Sir Richard to the study, where he took up his position behind the desk and looked at her with pale, chilly eyes.

"We have, I think, allowed you a good deal of freedom, have we not?"

"Yes, Sir Richard." Her heart felt heavy as lead.

"But you knew that there were parts of the house in which you were not expected to go?"

Frances flushed. Had someone seen her on the family bedroom floor? "Yes," she said slowly.

"Then why did you choose to paint in here?"

Her bewilderment must have been plain, for Sir Richard said, "So you didn't. Then how do you account for this?"

He took a picture from the shelf behind him and a sheet of paper, then laid them on the desk in front of her.

Frances gasped. "I thought Mary was joking! She said

they were the same, but I thought she meant similar. I painted mine in the garden. Mr. Kennedy would be able to prove that. He used the shortcut that day and stopped to talk to me. He said these were roses from Versailles."

"I got up early this morning—I suffer now and again from sleeplessness—and came here to write letters. Mary was down seeing to the fires, and she had this with her, comparing it with the one Francesca Hallowes painted. Oh, she was treating it very carefully. She had a clean towel to protect it from any soot marks. I couldn't see any way it could have been so exact without your having copied it here. I'm afraid insomnia can make one testy as well as suspicious. I think I owe Mary an apology as well as yourself."

"You do believe me?"

"I think you aren't the sort of person to abuse a privilege. And the roses were first grown at Versailles."

Frances was silent. Though she hadn't intruded into the study, she had elsewhere, and wished that she could confess. "May I tell Mary you aren't still cross with her? She'll be so worried."

"I think so. But as for the coincidence—I still can't fathom that. There's a good deal about you that can't be fathomed. If I believed in such things, I'd say you were haunted. But why you?"

Frances shook her head without speaking.

"She did die untimely, poor child," Sir Richard said, almost to himself. "And there are no letters—nothing to say—nothing, at least, that I've uncovered. Run along, then, Frances, and take your painting with you. It's something you can be proud of, however you came to produce it."

It wasn't until she was out of the room that Frances

thought of Martin. He must be all right, as his father would be very unlikely to place the mystery of the rose picture above the health of his only child. She could feel no sense of relief, only a violent disappointment. She must have used too little of the laudanum. Or perhaps Martin hadn't yet drunk the ginger beer. The thought chilled her.

She went upstairs to replace the painting, and her room seemed tainted with memories of Martin's intrusion. Looking at her wrist, she saw that it was bruised. All of her horror and fear of him returned, and she experienced a longing to run out into the grounds and breathe fresh air. But rain was now streaming over the panes and the branches were obscure, shadowy things out of a nightmare.

She ran down to look for Mary.

CHAPTER ELEVEN

The rain slackened after lunch, and Frances put on her boots
and fetched her umbrella, longing to be alone. Aunt Bessie
had grumbled about having to take Martin his breakfast, and
Frances's heartbeats had quickened at the sound of his name.

"How did he seem today?"

"Quiet, but that won't last long. Years may his father
live, for there's no one here would wish that young man to
be master. That reminds me, there'll be a young lass, one of
the Brodies, who'll be coming this afternoon for an interview
for the new position. She'll take Mary's place, and Mary'll
take Jenny's."

"Jenny's?"

Aunt Bessie set her lips. "Jenny—wasn't suitable."

"Oh." Frances wasn't supposed to know about that. "But
I'm pleased Mary's got a step up the ladder. I like Mary."

Her aunt gave a half-approving grunt and went about her
business, her starched apron rustling.

Outside, the air was warm and damp, and the bits of

Frances's hair that escaped began to curl against her brow and neck. Drops of rain fell from the wet foliage to thump upon the opened umbrella. She walked around the house toward the edge of the gorge she had noticed from her aunt's sitting-room window.

Standing at a discreet distance from the slippery edge, she saw how deep the ravine was and how, in the past, large pieces of rock had become detached, falling to the bottom in a jagged heap partly overgrown with moss and lichen. Long ago, a fence had been erected, but only a few broken and rotted stumps remained. It seemed sad that the house would, in time, suffer the same fate if Mrs. Kennedy was right about the scarcity of money to effect repairs. The gatehouse had, after all, very nearly disappeared.

It was quiet here, no sounds of birdsong—only the soft, secret patter of the heavy drops onto the earth. Frances wondered if it would be raining in France, where her father was. She remembered Willie McKenzie's descriptions of the trenches and felt sick.

Then, quite suddenly, she knew she wasn't alone. The ring, icy cold, stung her neck and she jerked, one foot slipping on the wet grass.

"You should be more careful," Martin reproved, his voice as cold as the ring.

She refused to look at him or to show her fear.

"What did you put into the ginger-beer bottle?" he asked.

"What makes you think I did that?" she summoned up the courage to ask.

"It didn't taste right."

"Complain to the village shop," she retorted with a boldness she didn't feel.

"It's never tasted like that before."

"You stole the bottle. It wasn't meant for you and you know it!"

"Do I? It strikes me that you're far cleverer than I imagined. You know a great deal more than you should. And you take sides." His voice was no longer cold but rough around the edges and becoming angry. "Other people's sides."

"I don't know what you're talking about," she said with assumed carelessness. "It was peaceful here before you came. Go away again, please."

"It's not for you to order me about! This is my land."

"It's your father's, and he's quite happy to let me use it while I'm here. He said so."

Martin came closer. Frances thrust out her hand so that he could see her wrist. "If you touch me again, I'll show this to your parents. They aren't fools. They'll recognize fingerprints."

He smiled nastily. "You've come to a bad place. It's especially dangerous in wet weather."

She drew back fearfully, the gulf seeming deeper than ever. "Aren't you supposed to be working?" she asked, her lips dry.

"Mama thought I needed fresh air."

"You'll be expected back soon. Your father's not so lenient." She willed her voice not to shake.

"Yes, Papa," Martin said softly, and there was something in his face that made Frances even more afraid. "As you say, he's—unfriendly."

"He isn't with me."

"That could change if I wanted it enough. If I don't get the ring, for instance."

155

"You can't complain about that to anyone else without rather awkward explanations."

Martin was silent, and the dark look he'd put on for his father was now directed toward herself. Frances began to edge away from him, and he laughed. He seemed tall and strong as a man. She turned to run up the slope, but he was quicker than she was, pulling at her sleeve, dragging her backward.

She bit her lip to stifle a scream. This couldn't possibly be happening. It must be one of those startlingly vivid nightmares she'd had of late. But it felt all too real, the cold, hard clutch on her wrist, the feel of his chest against her back, his breath against her neck.

"Liar!" he said viciously. "You were wearing it all the time."

She realized that her blouse had slipped during the struggle, exposing the back of her neck and the chain. Worse still, she knew that they were sliding slowly but steadily toward the brink, and that if some miracle didn't happen quickly, it wouldn't matter much about the Luck or, indeed, anything at all. Then her hand brushed a stub of a branch and she was holding a thick stem of a whinbush. Her fingers tightened about it, her hold reinforced by bringing up her other hand to encircle the tough hardness. The weight of Martin's body threatened to tear her fingers apart, and she kicked out in fright.

He cried out, then the intolerable strain was gone and she was flung forward onto spiky branches. Martin shouted again, his voice muted and distorted. Then there was a thud and a silence in which her heart struck hammer blows against her ribs. Slowly the knocking subsided, and she discovered that her hands hurt and that her stocking had been torn just below the knee.

Turning her head with infinite care, she saw that she was only a foot from the edge. Her eyes slid to the corners and she was staring into the gulf.

Martin lay spread-eagled close-by the edge of the rock pile, and there was blood on the nearest stone.

She remembered screaming thinly, working her way around the whinbush and crawling upward to join the slithery path that led down in erratic bends to the floor of the gorge. Mud sucked at her boots. Her hands and clothing were smeared with the wet earth.

Staring down at Martin, she saw that his face was white and his eyes closed. For once, Martin hadn't been careful enough.

It took two or three minutes for the unbidden thought to assume its true importance. Then she cried out, "Simon? Simon! This is your only chance! You must take it. Do you hear?"

Her shaking fingers fumbled for the chain, snapping it open to release the ring. It slid onto her finger, a circlet of ice and fire. Staring deeply into the wastes of the red desert, her eyes searched for any trace of a human figure, but there was nothing. She turned the ring so that she saw the shadowy gorge with the snaking water at its foot. Simon was there, Francesca at his shoulder. Then the tiny forms became large as life and so close that she could have touched them.

"Martin fell," she said, her voice high and strained. "You don't think—he's dead? I haven't touched him. If he is, you'll never get back, will you? Please say he isn't."

157

"He's not dead," Simon told her, so positively that she knew it must be true.

"Then do it," she urged, her face white. "Do it now, whatever it is you have to do."

"Yes," Francesca was whispering. "You have to. You've waited so long. Dear Simon, you have to. I won't be far away. I'll never be far away, ever again."

Frances closed her eyes, which had become heavy with fatigue. Struggling to open them again, she fancied she saw a faint mist play over Martin's face, hiding his features. Weariness sent her to her knees, then she was falling sideways, the mist curling about her, her head beginning to spin, her thoughts floating away like a leaf on the burn, then lost in the shadowy caverns of her mind.

"Miss Frances? Miss Frances!"

It sounded like Mary's voice, only queerly hollow as though she were around a corner of a cave.

Frances tried to struggle toward the voice.

"Oh, don't move, miss," Mary said from much closer, the echoing ring gone from her tone. "It's as much as my job's worth to be caught here with you half out of bed."

"Bed?" Frances opened her eyes and found herself in a strange room with green-and-white wallpaper, a carved plaster cornice depicting fruit and leaves, and a view of foliage drowned in rain. Mary was staring between polished rosewood bed poles, her forehead furrowed with anxiety.

Frances tried to pull herself up against the frilled pillow that smelled of lavender, but her body felt strangely weak. Green chintz curtains were looped behind her head. Even the raindrops on the panes seemed faintly tinged with green.

"Where on earth?" she queried weakly.

"Oh, miss," Mary said, with the ghost of a smile. "I'm that pleased to hear your voice. Truly I am—"

"Where am I?"

"In the guest room. It wasn't so far to carry you and easier for the doctor."

"Doctor?"

"You was found in the gorge with Master Martin."

"Martin! Martin—fell."

"Sir Richard saw the marks in the mud where both of you slipped, then where you went down to see to him."

Frances was silent for a moment. Then she said, "How is he?"

"Hasn't come around yet. Look, I'm not supposed to be in this room. I'm doing Jenny's work, and I'm really meant to be next door, only I was that anxious. I should tell her ladyship you're awake, only she'd want to know why I was here."

"Say you heard me calling out."

Mary's face lightened. "You *must* be all right if you can think *that* quick!"

"Of course I am. I suppose I must have fainted with the shock of seeing Martin by the rocks."

"I'll tell them you're all right now." Mary bustled away.

As soon as she'd gone, the strange bedchamber began to feel oppressive. Frances discovered a yearning to be in her own attic room with the sound of the dripping tap and the scrape of the branches against the high window. She began to wonder how they'd been found and whether or not Martin would still be himself when he came out of his swoon. Breathlessly, she tried to envisage what might happen next, but could see no end to the situation.

Her fingers felt cold and she began to rub them together, producing a sound like that of taffeta skirts rustling. She lifted her hands and stared. The Luck was no longer there. Her spirits plummeted. Almost the last thing she could recall with any clarity was looking into the depths of the ring and seeing the tiny encapsulated figures of Simon and Francesca become mysteriously life-sized and close enough to touch.

Footsteps were approaching, and she experienced a moment of panic. How could she explain why she had been wearing the Halloweses' talisman, supposedly buried in the silt of the black pool? The steps of her discovery of the ring flashed through her mind: the weathercock on the church steeple spinning and glinting over the gravestones, the thorny wood that had torn spitefully at her skirts, the little, half-buried box kicked from its hiding place. Visions of a scarlet desert and the purple sky, the gorge drowned in night's blue shadows. Simon—

The door swung open and Sir Richard and Lady Hallowes stood in the gap, pale-faced, their eyes questioning.

She waited, anguished, for some word of reproach.

Lady Hallowes came forward. There were shadows under her eyes and her face was strained. "Thank God one of you is all right. What happened?"

No mention of the Luck, Frances thought, dizzy with relief. She realized suddenly that she felt stronger than she'd ever been, strong enough to cope with whatever life had to offer, good or bad.

She wondered what to say about the fall. If she told the truth, Sir Richard at least would stop caring for his son, and

160

if her prayers were answered, the boy who was Martin would awake as Simon. Simon must not be vilified for what his brother had wished to do.

"I was looking for the gorge. I could see it from Aunt Bessie's sitting-room window but not from my own. But I forgot about the mud. I started to slip and I suppose I must have shouted for help. And Martin came."

"The marks of your boots were so deep," Sir Richard said, and Frances sensed his suspicion.

"I remember I was very frightened. I may have struggled. Then I caught hold of the whin, and suddenly I'd stopped sliding. Martin mustn't have been prepared for such an abrupt stop. I'm sorry that he's hurt."

"He didn't come—looking for you?"

"Why should he, Sir Richard? I hardly knew him."

"There were bruises on your wrists."

"He tried to catch me."

"They looked—older."

"Richard," Lady Hallowes remonstrated, her face white and pinched, "one would think you were trying to lay something bad at Martin's door. Frances is above all a truthful girl. Why should she lie?"

"Why, indeed."

They looked down at her, neither truly satisfied. That would change when the boy in the bed in Martin's room came out of his swoon.

"How is Martin?"

"Still out of his senses, but we are assured that no bones are broken. There's an injury to his head, and that's what worries us. The doctor will be coming back soon and will want to speak to you."

161

"I'm all right, really I am. I must get up."

"No, you must not!" Lady Hallowes told her. "I'll have someone fetch you a little soup and toast. If you feel better tomorrow, then that's different."

"It couldn't have been a pleasant experience," Sir Richard said. "You are bound to feel a reaction. The doctor's gone to the McKenzies. It seems that Willie is worrying about something he said to you, and his mother is full of apologies."

"I don't suppose he meant it. He was feeling wretched and no wonder. It's hard for him to be as he is."

"It must be hard for you," Sir Richard pointed out. "But I suspect Willie'll have something more friendly to say next time you meet."

Frances flushed, then with a certainty she couldn't explain, said, "I'm sure Papa will be all right."

"We very much hope so, my dear."

"Yes, we do," Lady Hallowes echoed, a strand of her dark red hair detached and hanging against the white column of her neck. She looked no more substantial than she had in her unreal room. Frances wondered if she'd been any different before the loss of her son. Perhaps when she sensed the change in Martin she'd become more alive, more responsive.

If there was any change in Martin! The thought brought a touch of coldness Frances couldn't repress.

The Halloweses left, and she heard them in the next room, their voices muted as though they wished not to disturb whoever was there. She must be next door to Martin's bedroom.

She waited in an agony of suspense for them to go. Francesca's voice seemed to be whispering, "I'm here."

Frances got out of bed. Her legs felt unsteady and she

162